DISCARD

SHADOW
THEATRE

SHA

FIONA CHEONG

DOW
THEATRE

a novel

SOHO

Published by
Soho Press, Inc.
853 Broadway
New York NY 10003

Library of Congress Cataloging-in-Publication Data
Cheong, Fiona.
Shadow theatre : a novel / Fiona Cheong.
    p. cm.
ISBN 1-56947-287-4 (alk. paper)
1. Women—Singapore—Fiction. 2. Singapore—Ficiton.
    I. Title.
PR9570.S53 C469 2002
823'.914—dc21   2002017565

10 9 8 7 6 5 4 3 2 1

Text design by Pauline Neuwirth, Neuwirth & Associates

DEDICATION

*To Danny and Leela Sofía
and in memory of my sister*

CONTENTS

*G*EOGRAPHICALLY LOCATED ONE *degree and eight minutes north of the Equator, the island of Singapore, once part of the land mass of the Malay Peninsula, is separated from the tip of the peninsula by a narrow strait and buffered by smaller islands from the full blast of seasonal monsoon winds. Possessing a natural harbor and situated at a confluence of the old trade routes between East and West, Singapore was colonized by the British in 1819, taken over by the Japanese in 1942, and returned to the British in 1945. Colonial rule ended in 1955, when Singapore became the only predominantly Chinese state in the Federation of Malaya. Due to irreconcilable differences in governmental philosophy between the Malays and the Chinese in power, Singapore was expelled from the Federation in 1965 and*

forced to re-form itself as an independent nation.

Modern scholars cannot verify the origin of the Sanskrit name "Singapura," or "Lion City," knowing only that it came into use sometime at the end of the fourteenth century because until then Chinese and Javanese seafarers referred to the island as Temasek. The Chinese trader Wang Ta-yuan, in particular, reported a settlement of pirates on the savage Tan-ma-shi, among whom were Chinese inhabitants who lived and dressed in native style.

The seventeenth-century Sejarah Melayu, or Malay Annals, on the other hand, attribute the rise of civilization on the island to Raja Chulan, an Indian warrior-king and descendant of Alexander the Great, who encamped at Temasek on his way to conquer China. Raja Chulan married the daughter of the god of the sea, who gave birth to a son, Sang Utama, who later became Prince of Palembang, the Sumatran city from which he then ruled the Buddhist maritime kingdom of Srivijaya.

According to the Sejarah Melayu, Sang Utama was forced to take refuge at Temasek one day during a storm. Sailing into the estuary of the present Singapore River, he encountered a strange beast with a red body, a black head, and a white breast, which he took to be a lion. Thinking the encounter a good omen, Sang Utama decided to build a trading city at its site. It was he who renamed the island Singapura. His city blossomed, but by 1365, under the rule of a successor, Singapura fell to the Javanese and was claimed as a vassal state of the empire of Majapahit.

It should be noted that neither the Sejarah Melayu nor the private papers of descendants of the earlier seafaring settlers are to be found among the official records stored in the various archives of the old British empire. The following pages, culled from such unofficial sources, tell of a race of women who still speak the language of the dreamer, who write in a saltwater wind, and breathe like the changing light over the sea.

No historically verifiable record exists of the events they report.

OCCURRENCES ON THE
FIRST AND SECOND
FRIDAYS IN

august 1994

SUSANNA WANG

daughter of kenneth and alice wang

father deceased

WE HAD HEARD about the diamond woman since forever, the syllables of her name blowing about the still air on slow weekday afternoons, just out of reach behind the yam and pandan leaves spreading along the cemetery's edge across from our windows. We were living in those days off River Road (which has since been renamed, perhaps for reasons having nothing to do with what happened that August, the month Mrs. Nair's daughter came home, but as our neighbors used to say, who's to know the government's reasons?). Our road itself had two names, as it was shaped like the alphabet U and met up with

River Road twice. Jo and I lived along the leg of the U facing the cemetery, with our back gardens lined up against the back gardens of houses along the other leg. But nobody we knew used either name much (only with strangers or when Jo and I were filling out forms at school), and mostly you'd hear one neighbor saying to another, "Supposed to be someone from our road-lah," or "Come, let's go home," as if in those days, everyone looked upon each other as almost family, and the aluminum fences and hedges of hibiscus and morning glory separating our gardens were a mere illusion.

And perhaps they were. Whispers floated through doors and windows every day, hushed gossip and speculative references spinning ceaselessly in the heat like ceiling fans while shirts were being washed or ironed, or the vegetables chopped and the meat pounded and seasoned for dinner. Women like the diamond woman seemed always to have existed, their faces unknown while the details of their deeds drifted up and down the road again and again, flattened facts like catechism lessons unwavering in their warning to us never to take anything for granted or trespass into the forbidden, because black magic was not a game and life wasn't meant to be perfect.

Someone might begin, "Eh, you hear about that woman? She took her own son to see the bomoh?" or, "You remember that woman? Her husband, caught with the waitress sitting in his lap?" Whoever was listening would nod, sometimes add solemnly, "Ah, ya-lah, you see some people, they never learn." And if you waited and stayed out of sight (in case there was talk of sex deemed unfitting for children to hear), one by one the stories would break loose, unleashed like a monsoon flood, recent stories and old stories or old stories with new details uncovered or reconfigured, all always secondhand as none of our neighbors was ever a witness or would want to confess to being one. Eventually, occasionally, a neighbor would get around to the diamond woman's story, even though it was a story retold so much, there didn't seem anything anyone could do to it to shed light on what may have happened. And yet, "Remember," someone might say, "itu woman, she kept complaining how her hubby went out every night, he didn't come home sampai two or three in the morning, she was afraid he would leave her for another girl, and then tengok-lah, look what happened."

What had happened was that the bomoh had put a diamond in the woman's cheek, inserted the glittering stone beneath the skin and left it there, like a pimple, and then the woman was given medicine to mix with her husband's coffee in the morning. But the woman was careless handling the medicine, or perhaps she had mixed up the bomoh's instructions, confusing the order of steps to be taken. The husband, instead of falling back in love with his wife, had fallen in love with their daughter. (Nobody knew how old the daughter was at the time. Charlotte's mother thought she might have been sixteen or seventeen, but Jo had overheard her mother saying to someone on the phone that Auntie Coco thought the girl wasn't even menstruating yet, and Auntie Coco was supposed to have a sixth sense about these things.) So the diamond woman had returned to the bomoh, frightened and pleading for medicine to alter her mistake, but as it turned out, not even the bomoh could undo the effect of the woman's own actions. The woman's only comfort was that as long as she kept the diamond in her cheek, her husband would not leave her. This was what the bomoh promised her. But it would always be their daughter whom he desired, because the bomoh had given the woman one of her strongest medicines.

So the story would go, each time it was retold.

That August Jo was fifteen and I was fourteen, and there were boys prowling about our daily lives (although mostly it was Jo whom they found sexy) and I wondered more than ever who the diamond woman was, how close by she lived or whether she had moved to a neighborhood farther away to save face, whether she was related to anyone we knew. I wondered who all those women were, who had "refused to take up their crosses" (as my mother would say at times when Jo's mother came over and they sat chatting in the kitchen), those women who had sought cures beyond the scope of priests or marriage counselors or psychiatrists, daring to visit the house that sat behind the back wall in the cemetery for powders and tea leaves to turn themselves beautiful, potions to freeze a vagabond lover's wandering gaze, Lucky Draw digits for a favorite son. I wondered about the missing details in their stories, the absence of names and dates that set them apart and left them adrift in a strand of gossip different from the usual.

All that no longer exists, or so it would appear if you were to return to our road now. You would see people's houses still there, bought up mostly by modern Singaporeans with advanced technological tastes and impatient minds, Singaporeans who used to live elsewhere on the island or in the wider world and remember nothing about us. And as for the few of our neighbors who remain, ask them about the stories, about the diamond woman, and what happened after Shakilah Nair came home, and they will most likely say it was all just rumor in the end.

And some of it was rumor, but that doesn't mean it didn't happen, and it's not as if everything that happened ever became a story.

There was the thing Jo and I and the other girls who were in the cemetery saw, a week before Shakilah Nair was supposed to arrive, which we've kept to ourselves because we couldn't tell what we were doing in the cemetery in the first place, and the truth was, we were cowards, all of us except for Jo (who kept the secret for my sake and for Fay's, even months later when we heard about the baby).

We were six yards from the bomoh's house, and Charlotte

had just emptied the packet of powder into the granite bowl . . .

Phillipa was there, and our new classmate Fay Timmerman (who was from Jakarta and was staying with her uncle on River Road, next door to the doctor's abandoned house).

Charlotte would want me to say it wasn't her, that it was one of the other girls who had volunteered to mix the powder, maybe even that it was me. But it was Charlotte who had procured the powder in the first place. Jo and I were responsible for the bowl (Jo having smuggled it out of her mother's kitchen that morning because Charlotte had insisted that it be a granite bowl), and Phillipa and Fay had brought an unopened box of white votive candles, and matches.

We had come over together after that Tuesday's choir practice, and Charlotte still smelled of incense from the sacristy because she had met Alphonsus Wong for a brief kissing rendezvous (while the rest of us had waited for her outside the church, Phillipa and I because no boys were attracted to either of us yet, Fay because she was new and nobody knew her, and Jo because she wasn't interested in dating boys from the choir, who tended also to be altar boys). You could smell the myrrh and rose oil in Charlotte's hair as she crouched over the bowl and got herself ready to mix the powder, which had to be done with her left index finger and very, very slowly. I was kneeling closest to her, on her right. Jo was next to me on my right, and on Jo's right was Phillipa, then Fay (who had lit the candles after they were arranged, each balanced firmly in a depression in the ground, one candle behind each of us). We were an almost complete circle, with one opening for the spirit that might join us.

Charlotte had given us the bomoh's instructions and we had followed them to a T. (Even Fay knew about the diamond woman, knew the possible consequences of the slightest deviation.) I say this so you'll see there were no mistakes, at least not on our part.

What was supposed to happen was that while Charlotte was mixing the powder, the reddish grains would grow warmer and warmer, swirling into shades of violet and maroon and deepening until the powder liquefied, after which point we were supposed to turn our heads and look around (one at a time), to see among the trees and gravesites the passing figures of our future husbands, maybe even their faces. (Faces weren't guaranteed, but you were supposed to be able to discern from a man's gait what kind of man he was, whether he was thoughtful and attentive and inclined to be faithful, or whether his soul was constantly unsettled, constantly in search of greener pastures.)

We weren't the first ever to try this ritual, or game, as the nuns used to call it. Nobody seems to play it anymore. People leave the spirits alone now, or perhaps it's true what some believe, that our energy is too interrupted by the noises and electricity breaking daily across the island, this perennial slam and crash of unending construction.

Still, you might hear more if you try. Be very quiet, breathe very slowly. It's possible if you'll let yourself, if you'll leave hold of where you are and come to where we used to be, smell us returning like sleep, the air dripping with frangipani and jasmine and fruit, with guava, mango and mangosteen, and florid, hairy husks of rambutans, promising the most delectable juice.

We had never seen Shakilah Nair, or her photograph, so nobody thought of her at the time. Aware only that someone was watching us as Charlotte was about to mix the powder, Jo turned to see who it was, and that was when she saw a pretty Eurasian woman smiling at her, about ten feet away, underneath a banyan tree. I heard Jo gasp, but when the rest of us looked, the woman was already walking away, and through the trees we could see she wasn't alone.

There was a child with her, a girl younger than we were, who was holding her hand. They were heading towards the bomoh's house, and then they disappeared, vanished like night into the sun as they passed the yellow shrine (the one sheltering a baby's grave).

That was why we didn't finish the ritual. Jo wasn't afraid, and I was willing to continue, but neither of us wanted to mix the powder, so when Charlotte changed her mind and Phillipa and Fay didn't volunteer, the afternoon was over.

MALIKA WAS OPENING the windows in Madam's living room when she saw the girl. Or rather, what caught her eye and made her pause long enough to set the new copper kettle shrieking like an emergency alarm on the kitchen stove was Madam's friend, dressed in a pair of Madam's sleeveless pajamas, pale green with flecks of white petals (because it had been a last-minute idea for the friend to spend the night), slipping into the house through the sliding glass doors of the study, which was the room Madam had added on to the house for herself back in 1985, after the children were all married and Madam's husband had passed away.

Since it was half-past five in the morning, the air still bluey bluey and crisp as dead leaves and noisy with calling birds, as Malika would describe it (as if Sali and I wouldn't have been awake ourselves at half-past five in the morning, but then that was how Malika talked, fancying herself our storyteller), and since Madam and her friend had stayed up quite late chatting (Madam with her usual bedtime glass of whiskey and the friend sipping iced water with lime because, as Malika had heard her telling Madam, she was almost in her sixth month), Malika was surprised to see the friend up so early, which was not to say she was expecting anything odd to happen, not on such an ordinary morning, and she herself had been doing nothing unusual, just going around the house, opening Madam's windows to let in the fresh air, as was her routine every morning, ever since Madam had started closing the windows at night.

The study extended from the side of the house, towards the back where Madam's bedroom was. It wasn't that far from the living room, but we agreed with Malika that it was possible Madam's friend hadn't noticed her or heard her unlocking the iron clasp on the windows. I remember there was a mango tree growing outside the living room, close to the windows. It could have blocked Malika from sight with its thick trunk. Or perhaps Madam's friend was so plagued by her dilemma that morning, over the book she was writing (she was a novelist, like Charlotte Brönte and Danielle Steele), she wasn't noticing anything around her.

"That's why I thought she didn't notice the girl," said Malika, when she was telling us about it.

I hadn't told her or Sali what else I knew about Madam's friend. I wasn't going to tell them, in case Madam found out that I had and thought of me as a busybody. At the moment, I was just one of Malika's friends, and perhaps because Madam was both kind and not paying attention to us, Sali and I were free to come and go as we pleased. No need to rock the boat, as I saw it.

So all Malika knew was what she remembered, coupled with some new details given to her by Madam (who from then on, particularly after what was about to happen had happened and her friend's visit started fading just like her daughters and her marriage into a sealed and sweetened past, would glow with both pride and sorrow whenever she reminisced about the days when Miss Shakilah had been a pupil at St. Agnes, and Madam had taught her, because as she would tell Malika, she both hoped and didn't hope she had had a hand in moulding Miss Shakilah into the success she had become in America—a famous writer and a university professor on top of that).

Needless to say, Madam herself didn't address Miss Shakilah as *Miss Shakilah* when the two of them were in conversation. That was only how she would refer to her in front of Malika. With Miss Shakilah directly, Madam would say, *Shak, my dear,* or *Darling, you don't understand,* with the same tenderness in her voice as when she was speaking on the phone with Caroline or Michelle (the eldest one, Francesca, was a stockbroker in London and never called home, although like the other two, she would fly back with Madam's grandchildren once a year, usually during the Christmas holidays, and as with the other two, sometimes the husband would come along and sometimes not).

Malika thought Madam could not have seen the girl in the garden because she was taking a shower at the time, although when Sali asked if she was sure about that, Malika couldn't say she was. "Madam always takes her shower at that time," was as close as Malika could get to pinpointing where Madam may have been at half-past five, somewhere else in the house or in the study with Miss Shakilah.

The girl looked Chinese, around nine or ten years old, and was standing behind Madam's sugar cane near the fence. Malika saw her after Miss Shakilah had stepped into the study, while Miss Shakilah was pulling the glass door shut (Malika could hear the rubbery glide of the door in its steel groove just before the kettle started whistling). The girl was very thin, her arms bony like bamboo. Malika wasn't sure at first if there was really someone there, until a small breeze came and the sugar cane leaves swayed a little to the left, and the girl didn't move.

Her stillness was also what aroused Malika's suspicion, because since when did a child ever stay still of her own accord? Having been with Madam since the birth of the second one, Caroline, Malika knew how little girls were if they were left free, if they weren't boxed away into sugar and spice and everything nice.

But the kettle was whistling (Malika hadn't known it was that sort of kettle, since Madam had just taken it out of the shopping bag yesterday when they had heard the doorbell ring, and in her excitement over seeing her friend, Madam had forgotten to tell Malika, and as usual, Malika had thrown away the box without reading it).

By the time she had turned off the stove and returned to the living room to look out of the windows again, the girl was gone.

IT WAS ON Wednesday that Malika saw the girl, and Friday when she told us, so Sali and I believed the gist of her story and wondered only what Malika might have embellished, not what she might have forgotten (as would happen at times with her other stories, the ones involving Madam's daughters, for instance, or stories about Madam and her husband, which Malika could never tell the same way twice). I had every Friday afternoon off and Sali had it every other week, so we had gone over to Madam's house as usual, taking the eight o'clock bus to Bukit Timah from Changi Road. (That bus didn't turn onto River Road. Sali wished it did but I didn't mind, as it was only a twenty-five-minute walk for us to the Changi Road bus stop, and then less than an hour's ride almost directly to Madam's house). Malika wasn't off on Fridays, but it was just as if she were, since Madam was at school until six o'clock, leaving us the whole house to ourselves. (Other days, Madam would come home between half-past three and four o'clock, but on Fridays the school choir met for practice and Madam was in charge of the choir, as she had been ever since she had started teaching thirty-three years ago. In fact, the choir was what had kept her going after Michelle got married and left, the last one.)

"She probably saw you and ran off before you could catch her," suggested Sali, as she lifted the lid on one of Madam's jewelry boxes to find her favorite brooch of Madam's, a small diamond peacock about to spread its feathers. (Madam kept it in the red lacquered box that sat on the left side of the dressing table, behind the photograph of her grandsons, Francesca's and Caroline's children, which had been taken during Michelle's wedding in 1981, two years before Madam's husband started complaining about his headaches. Sali always went for the peacock, sooner or later, when we were at the house. We saw no harm in it, since Madam herself had worn the brooch only once, perhaps because it was the last thing her husband had bought for her on his own. Madam's husband had given her the peacock for their silver wedding anniversary. After that, everything had gone downhill, his health plummeting like a pebble kicked off a precipice, although as Malika remembered, the signs were there even before the first diagnosis, before anyone was willing to see them).

"How could she have run off so fast? I didn't even hear the gate opening or closing," she said, responding to Sali's implication that perhaps the girl was just a neighbor's unruly child. "Don't tell me she just slipped out between the bars. As thin as she was, no child is that thin."

"You go and look at the gate," said Sali, even though she knew how long Malika had been with Madam, and how many times she had opened and closed the gate for Madam's husband if it was raining when he came home from work.

"You go and look yourself," said Malika, and she picked up one of Madam's hairbrushes and tapped Sali on the back of the head with it. (She was sitting on a square stool near the dressing table, while I was on Madam's bed, away from the dressing table and the jewelry, remaining as uninvolved as possible in all of this.) Sali laughed, with the peacock glittering on her blouse like an extra giggle, pinned just above her breast. She looked at Malika in the mirror, and then they both looked at me.

Malika put down the hairbrush and reached for Madam's diamond bracelet, which was lying on top of another red lacquered box (they were a set of three, brought back long ago from a vacation in Hong Kong). She held the bracelet up to the dusty sunrays coming through Madam's bedroom window to her right, and Sali turned her head and stared at the circle of diamonds dangling from Malika's finger as if she had never seen them before, as if we didn't do this every few months (she and Malika going through Madam's jewelry to see if anything new had shown up, while I kept my ears open for the sound of Madam's car, in case she came home unexpectedly, which had happened twice so far).

"What do you think, Lu?" asked Malika, as she slipped the bracelet over Sali's right wrist and locked the tiny gold clasp.

"You mean, about the girl?" I asked, although of course that was what she meant.

"Yes, the girl." Malika turned her head towards me as Sali lifted her hand and pretended to brush her hair back with her fingers, the bracelet sliding like a ring of stars against her skin in the mirror.

"I don't know what to think," I said. "If it wasn't a real girl, why would she be appearing now? And why here?"

"Ya-lah, if this were a haunted house, you would have found out long before this," said Sali, taking a few steps back from the dressing table. She nodded and smiled at her reflection in the mirror. Then, slowly, she stretched out her hand, as if someone else had reached for it and was lifting it to his lips to kiss her fingers, Western style, probably the Hollywood film director Sali believed she was destined to meet one day, who would fall in love with her and whisk her away to California, where she would become the next Marilyn Monroe. (I'm not saying Sali had a plan. But she was still young enough to believe in her hopes and dreams.) I watched as she touched the diamonds on her wrist, her lips moving as if she were explaining to the film director, the fellow who had kissed her fingers, how the bracelet had once belonged to her grandmother and how she, Sali, would wear it now and then to draw her grandmother's spirit near. (Sali had heard from Madam Albuquerque's daughter that Westerners were gullible about stories like that.) She was only twenty-three on this afternoon, five years younger than I, without a serious boyfriend in sight but several hopeful ones in tow.

Both of us were younger than Malika, who was closer to Madam's age, and Madam, I remember, would celebrate her fifty-sixth birthday that November. Malika was eleven years younger, although neither of them showed it. (Now that Madam's husband, who had married her when she was nineteen, was gone, Madam was starting to gather her share of broken hearts, even at her age. Malika couldn't believe how persistent some old men could be, including those who didn't have much to offer Madam, not even their own real teeth.)

She would have been forty-five on the morning she saw the girl. Forty-five and unmarried, a fact as plain and simple as the single bead Malika wore on a thin gold chain around her neck, the oval red bead holding for her a sentimental value, as she put it, and since it was obvious she didn't want to say more, we had left it at that. What I remember is that Malika had never worried openly about whether she was ever going to have the chance to have her own baby. Caroline and Michelle were like her own children, she would say, and even when we didn't ask her about it, from time to time Malika would remind us out of the blue that Francesca, too, always brought something back for her when she visited, and so what was there to regret? Yet, the fact that she was forty-five and unmarried may have been why the girl had chosen her.

Malika had turned her attention back to Sali, who was continuing to woo the film director after he had kissed her fingers.

A wind blew into the room as Sali tilted back her head and laughed into the mirror. Outside, some branches in Madam's garden creaked, probably those in the two banyan trees, which were the trees nearest that part of the house.

I felt a bird fly past the window. Or rather, I saw out of the corner of my eye what I thought could only be a bird's body, flying across the sun in the window. Malika must have felt it, too. She turned her head at once, but the bird was already gone.

Sali, from the looks of it, was too busy seducing her film director to notice anything. She was still talking, her lips still moving in the mirror as she invented for the fellow more stories about how her grandmother's ghost was always around to protect her (when in truth, Sali had been given away to an aunt shortly after she was born because of a fortuneteller's warning that her moon and her mother's moon would collide otherwise, and when this aunt, whom Sali had grown up calling her mother, had followed her husband, whom Sali had called her father, from Malacca to Singapore, Sali was only three years old, and that was the last time she had seen her grandmother). Malika and I watched as her right hand fluttered up to Madam's peacock. She caressed the diamond feathers, and then, as if she were innocently unaware of the blunt bulge straining in the fellow's pants, she let her fingers drop, coyly down her blouse, touching her nipple underneath in passing.

When Malika glanced up, she seemed startled to find me in the mirror.

Or perhaps I was mistaken about that.

WHAT MALIKA REMEMBERED about Miss Shakilah had to do with the two occasions on which Miss Shakilah had been at Madam's house before. Once was when Madam's whole class had come over at the end of the school year in 1973 (Malika remembered the heavy rain cascading off the tiled roof of the patio while the girls were serenading Madam with a song they had written to the musical score of *Top of the World*, which was popular that year and sung on cassettes by Karen Carpenter, the one who later became very sick and died), and the second time in 1979, also in December. That time, Miss Shakilah had come alone, looking a bit different from the first time because she was no longer twelve years old. By then, she had cut her hair (she used to wear plaits), and she had lost a lot of weight (not an ounce left of her puppy fat), and Malika would remember how the seat of Miss Shakilah's blue dungarees had hung off her backside with enough room for two fried chickens, as she put it.

Now, fifteen years later, Miss Shakilah didn't look so different from when she had left for America. (That was the reason for her second visit to Madam's house. She was gone two days later, on a late-night Pan American flight departing out of the new Changi Airport and destined for the John F. Kennedy Airport in New York City, via Hong Kong and Heathrow. What I've heard is that no one suspected it would be the last time anyone here would lay eyes on her for so many years, perhaps not even Miss Shakilah herself. Certainly, her mother was expecting her to come home during the summer holidays at first, and when that didn't happen, Miss Shakilah's mother had told herself, and anyone who asked about it, that her daughter was just busy with her studies and would return after getting her degree.

Not even Miss Shakilah's closest friend since childhood, her friend Rose, who had grown up with Miss Shakilah as if they were sisters, knew Miss Shakilah's actual reason for staying away, although because they had been so close, Rose did suspect it wasn't just Miss Shakilah's studies. Besides, Miss Shakilah had received her first degree in 1983, and another one, her master's, in 1985, both in English literature, and still she hadn't come home.)

That morning, she was talking in the kitchen with Madam until a quarter to seven, when Madam had to leave for school. (Madam had been driving herself ever since the family chauffeur's retirement shortly after her husband's passing. This was partly to save money, but also as Malika believed, Madam liked the new feel of independence that came with driving her own car. She had owned a driver's license since she was twenty-one, which she had kept renewing over the years, mostly in case there was an emergency and the chauffeur wasn't available. But in all the years that Malika had been with her, Madam had never driven her own car. Now she would take long drives by herself, along the new highway to the airport, where she would turn the car around and drive back. Malika thought it was because that was the longest drive possible in Singapore without traffic jams, as Madam had mentioned to her once. Which, by the way, was why Madam would leave for school at a quarter to seven, in case of a traffic jam, even though driving to St. Agnes usually took less than twenty minutes now that part of the drive was along the new highway. She wanted to be sure she was never late, because General Assembly started at half-past seven and she was in charge of the music. She was late once, on the morning her husband was taken to the hospital for the last time, but from what I've heard, it was only that once.)

Miss Shakilah and Madam had been discussing what to do about Miss Shakilah's dilemma, which they had started talking about in bits and pieces on the night before. (On the night before, they had talked mostly about their families, Madam asking about Miss Shakilah's mother (Miss Shakilah's father having passed away some time ago) and Miss Shakilah asking about Madam's daughters and the grandchildren. Miss Shakilah had known Madam's daughters in school, but none of them were exactly her age, so they wouldn't have been in the same classes. Francesca was a year older, Caroline was a year younger, and Michelle was four years younger. Francesca and Miss Shakilah could have been friends but Francesca hadn't been very sociable as a child, and as for Caroline, she had been so wild, dressing up and wearing lipstick and mascara even before her elder sister did. Miss Shakilah, when she was still a schoolgirl, hadn't shown a hint of wildness. Malika remembered her as Madam's favorite pupil for years. Bright, quiet, respectful. With the kind of curiosity that might kill a cat, Madam used to say. Her Shak could come up with questions no one else could think of. This was what Malika remembered, when she looked back upon some of her conversations with Madam in those years.)

From what Malika understood, Miss Shakilah's dilemma boiled down to her having too many voices in this latest novel. That was how Miss Shakilah had described the problem to Madam. Her publisher thought there were too many voices, or more precisely, too many storytellers. They made the story difficult to follow. This publisher wanted Miss Shakilah to revise the manuscript, cut the book down to three voices at the most. Miss Shakilah didn't want to do it. Leaving the book with only three voices would change the story entirely, she told Madam. Yet, how was she going to get the book published, otherwise? Her agent believed she would run into the same problem with most American publishers. Given her new state of affairs (the baby coming), she couldn't afford to be lackadaisical about money.

"Why are more than three voices so difficult to follow? Don't Americans know how to pay attention to several people talking at one time? They should come sit at a dinner table over here," Madam had pointed out, on the night before, while Malika had nodded her head in secret agreement. (It was the first time Malika had heard anyone discuss storytelling in such a serious way, and she had gleaned enough from the conversation to understand that this kind of discussion must happen often in America, or perhaps only in the university. She wondered what Miss Shakilah meant by her argument that fewer voices would change the story entirely. Malika always tried to leave room in her mind for things she might not be aware of due to her lack of sufficient formal education.)

"Americans aren't used to it, I guess. That's what my publisher thinks. My editor's afraid the book won't sell." Miss Shakilah had said this with a sigh, and then she had shrugged her shoulders loosely, as if it didn't really matter why the publisher thought there were too many voices. American publishers were impossible to argue with. That was what her sigh and shrug conveyed.

That was when Madam had invited Miss Shakilah to spend the night, so that they could both sleep on it and see if a solution presented itself in the morning. Given how late it was getting, especially (almost midnight). Taxi drivers would be charging double rates soon.

"Two heads are better than one," Madam had said, smiling a bit sheepishly at the cliché as she leaned forward on the sofa to clink glasses with Miss Shakilah.

So the night had ended, with Madam calling for Malika to close the windows while she found some pajamas and a new toothbrush for Miss Shakilah, and then Madam had turned on the air conditioner in Michelle's old bedroom, and she had given Miss Shakilah a foot massage with eucalyptus oil to help her relax.

But no solution had presented itself, after all.

Malika watched as Miss Shakilah rose from the table with her empty plate in her hands (both she and Madam had had two slices of buttered toast each, which, accompanied by black, sug-arless coffee, was Madam's usual breakfast). Sunlight from the window above the sink was pouring into the room, throwing long shallow beams across the black-and-white checkered floor (modeled after the kitchen floor of a hotel suite Madam and her husband had stayed in when they were in New York City in 1959, the year after Francesca was born and before Malika arrived). As Miss Shakilah put her plate down in the sink, Malika saw how slim her feet still were, but striped pale where the straps of her sandals had blocked the sun, making Miss Shakilah's feet look like the feet of any European tourist. Except for that, and except for her American accent, and the little extra weight gained because of her pregnancy, Malika thought Miss Shakilah seemed very much the same girl who had come to the house in the loose dungarees, with the same air of impatience in her movements as when she had hugged Madam fifteen years ago and said lightly, "See you in June."

"Miss, you can just leave it," Malika heard herself say, as Miss Shakilah stood a moment at the sink as if she were about to wash the plate.

Madam had left the kitchen and was in the dining room (where before Madam's husband had passed away, he and Madam used to have their meals but now, the dining table would be set only when her daughters and grandchildren visit-ed, or when Madam decided to throw a dinner party for her old friends, which happened occasionally, once or twice a year—"before they all keel over," Madam was fond of saying, with a wry smile). Malika could hear her gathering her papers and books for school, and then the lid of the piano that sat against the dining room wall closing with a soft thud. Madam was going to give Miss Shakilah a lift home on the way. "Come," she had said, and from outside the back door, while sorting out clothes to be put into the washing machine from clothes to be hand-washed, Malika had seen her stroke Miss Shakilah's forearm lovingly before she left the kitchen, "I'll take you to your mum's house."

(Madam had asked Miss Shakilah when they had first sat down to breakfast, what about getting the book published in Singapore. "You want me to ask around for you?" she had offered, and Miss Shakilah had replied, "I don't know," in a way that meant no, politely. Then with a sigh, Miss Shakilah had added, "I don't think publishers here pay much."

"Tell your editor this is how we tell stories," Madam had suggested, finally. "Ask him—him or her?"

"Her."

"Ask her to look at a piece of batik. Ah, that's what you should do, show her a piece of batik, how complicated and interwoven everything is. Maybe then she'll understand. What do you think?" Madam had so wanted to be of help, and Miss Shakilah had smiled, aware of this, and said she would try it, perhaps it would work.

Malika didn't know if Madam had heard in Miss Shakilah's tone another no. It was a quarter to seven by then and Madam had started getting up from the table.)

"Did you see her?" Miss Shakilah was asking, still at the sink. She was looking out of the window but not at anything in particular, Malika could tell.

"See who, Miss?"

"I think you know."

Malika thought at first that after so many cold American winters, Miss Shakilah was standing in front of the window so she could feel the heat on her face and neck (Miss Shakilah was wearing the yellow linen dress she had worn the day before, loosely fitting with short sleeves and a scoop neckline), but later Malika would wonder if perhaps she was wrong, if perhaps Miss Shakilah had been searching the garden for the girl, although the sugar cane was on the other side of the house and ghosts were often fussy about where they chose to appear.

"I saw you," she said, turning to Malika. "Earlier, when you were opening the windows. You must have seen her. Did you?"

There was a certain urgency in Miss Shakilah's voice, and Malika saw in Miss Shakilah's long-lashed brown eyes (still clear and bright but definitely older, definitely experienced, Malika thought now) an anxious glimmer, as if Miss Shakilah desperately wanted to hear that she, Malika, had seen the girl. What Malika wondered was how it had been possible for Miss Shakilah herself to have seen the girl, since the windows in Madam's study opened out towards the banyan trees and the back fence. There were no windows in the wall near the sugar cane. The only way was if Miss Shakilah had noticed the girl before going into the study, so Malika told herself that must have been what happened.

Only later would she realize, as she replayed the scene over and over in her mind, that there had been no one in the sugar cane when she had first looked through the glass of the living-room windows, when they were still closed.

"Yes, Miss," she said, in reply to Miss Shakilah's question. "The girl in the sugar cane, yes, I saw her. You know who she is, Miss?"

Miss Shakilah shook her head and smiled. "No, I don't," she told Malika.

There was sorrow in her smile, Malika thought at first, and then she wondered if she was mistaken, since there would be no reason for Miss Shakilah to feel sorrow over a child she didn't know, and Malika didn't get the feeling that Miss Shakilah was lying.

"Has Madam seen her?" asked Miss Shakilah, and Malika wasn't sure if she meant earlier that morning, or if Miss Shakilah was inquiring as to whether Madam knew there was a ghost in the garden?

She wondered why Miss Shakilah hadn't asked Madam about it herself, but there could have been any number of reasons. They hadn't seen each other in fifteen years and in a way, Miss Shakilah and Madam were just starting to get to know each other as friends. There was so much else for them to share about their present lives. And Miss Shakilah was preoccupied with worry about her book (and her baby). Or perhaps she didn't want to worry Madam, in the event that Madam hadn't seen the girl.

"No, Miss, I don't think so," said Malika, without clarifying for herself exactly what Miss Shakilah had meant by her last question because there was no time. She could hear Madam leaving the dining room, which was only a few footsteps away from the kitchen, down a small corridor with walls covered with photographs of the grandchildren growing up (there were seven now, the elder four boys and Michelle's three girls).

Madam's flat heels tapped lightly on the parquet floor as they came towards the kitchen. In less than half a minute, Madam was standing in the doorway, with a pink rattan bag slung over her right shoulder and a yellow one hanging from her left hand, both overstuffed with books and manila folders, and she was saying to Miss Shakilah, "Are you ready, darling?"

"Madam," Malika began, but Madam knew what she was about to say and was already waving Malika's words away with her right hand, her diamond ring sparkling on her wedding finger.

"Yes, I know, Malika. Tomorrow. Tomorrow afternoon, I'll go shopping for one of those travel carts. Okay?" She smiled and explained to Miss Shakilah, "Malika's so sweet, always worrying about me. Come, let's go."

"You tell her, Miss," Malika pleaded with Miss Shakilah before she left the room, and Miss Shakilah nodded and agreed to try to coax Madam into not carrying such heavy bags.

Neither of them mentioned the girl, almost as if that conversation hadn't occurred, but Malika could see on Miss Shakilah's face when she was walking out (although Miss Shakilah wasn't looking at her directly) a kind of relief, her features relaxing as if she understood something now, as if a curtain were beginning to rise and someone had lit a candle for her in the darkness ahead.

That was the feeling Malika was left with, as she removed the damp clothes from the washing machine and dropped them into the dryer (it was Francesca who had bought the washing machine and dryer and insisted that Malika learn to use them). She could hear Madam's car backing out of the driveway in the front of the house, then a pause, then the long, slow swing of the wrought-iron gate. Madam never called her out to close the gate for her anymore, not even when it rained.

ROSE SIM

daughter of sim hock siew and his wife helena

father deceased

CHANDRA SUBRINAYA. SHE'S probably changed her name by now, to her husband's name, whatever it is. Probably some kind of Western name, because Chandra was one of those, always hankering after the angmo boys. The blonder, the better, was her motto. Not that she would ever admit it, but it was obvious to anyone who wasn't blind. All you had to do in those days was wait around after her shift at the library was over, and see who came to pick her up. Without fail, it was always an angmo, usually American, since there were already a lot of Americans working in Singapore at the time, which was also why I thought Shak wouldn't find it so strange to be here—if she felt strange.

Chandra must have wondered about it herself, whether Shak was going to seek out the company of Americans, and what sort of competition that would be for her.

Of course it had occurred to me Shak might feel a tiny bit strange. Even if there was no reason for her to feel that way because she was from here, we don't always feel the way we should, right? Fifteen years. That's a long time to be away from anywhere, but especially where Singapore's concerned. We had changed a lot, you know. Our whole country was getting a facelift. Already, we had jumped from being the third busiest port in the world when Shak left to being the first, busier even than New York City or Amsterdam—imagine.

Luckily our neighborhood hadn't changed that much. Not yet, although some houses were being renovated along River Road, where new families had moved in. On our own road, Auntie Coco and her sister were the only neighbors Shak didn't know, since they had moved in in 1985, and by then, Shak had been gone for six years already. (The family that used to live in Auntie Coco's house had moved out after the grandmother died. For a few years the house had remained empty, so people were saying it was haunted by the grandmother's ghost. But then Auntie Coco and her sister had bought the house, and as my mother and her yakkity-yak friends were keen to point out, Auntie Coco hadn't tried to sell the house in all the time that she and her sister had been living in it, so the grandmother's ghost was just a rumor, in their opinion.)

And the old Muslim cemetery was still there, on our side of the granite wall that ran along the back of the cemetery, with Kampong Alam on the other side, where Che' Halimah lived. She and our mothers used to be classmates, you know. She, too, had once been a pupil at the convent. Che' Halimah, whom most people knew of only as the bomoh. She was still living that year, and I wondered if Shak would want to go and visit her, but I thought I wouldn't ask. In case the idea hadn't entered Shak's mind, I didn't want to put it there. With the old Shak, there would have been no question that she would want to see Che' Halimah, but we were much older now, not teenagers anymore, foolish and restless the way we used to be.

Shak, in particular, had to think for two, as they say.

It still looked the same, the cemetery, except that the hinges on the iron gate at the River Road entrance were so rusted now, no one bothered to try to close the gate anymore and it was always ajar. But the fence was still only on the River Road side. Along the side facing our houses there had never been a fence, and even though I remember people would talk about putting up some kind of barrier, no one had tried to do it. In our schooldays that was the side Shak would use to enter the cemetery, you know, right there in front of everyone's windows. Of course she would do it only at night, waiting until after people were supposed to be asleep. Then she would slip out of her house and cross the road. It was easier than walking down to River Road and all the way to the iron gate. Still, I wouldn't have taken that sort of risk if I were the one meeting boys in secret, to experiment with you know what, over by the baby's shrine, because they could find shelter there in case it rained.

No one else knew how reckless Shak could be. People around here always knew she was wild (only at the convent was anyone fooled into believing Shak was Miss Goody Two Shoes—Mrs. Sandhu for sure, our Secondary One form-mistress who had been Shak's favorite teacher the whole time we were in school—although of course the Sisters always knew the truth, about Shak, because you can't fool nuns, you know). But only I knew what Shak actually did, and what her limits were, because I was her best friend, her oldest and closest friend. That was why nowadays I had fallen into the habit of avoiding people from our past, which is not an easy thing to do in Singapore, but how else was I to save face? Because if someone were to ask me directly why Shak hadn't kept in touch with anyone—not even me—while she was in America, what could I say?

Fifteen years she was over there. And now, out of the blue, she was back. Pregnant and without a single sparkle on her finger. Not even an engagement ring—imagine.

Still, what was important was that she had come home at last. Not for good, but at least to visit. Let bygones be bygones, I kept telling myself.

True friendship never dies, you know.

SUSANNA WANG

TRY SEEING MR. DHARMA'S garden the way it was, not overgrown with neglect as it is now but ripe with rambutans and papayas where they hung, nestled richly in his trees, the grove of tall, green sugar cane that leaned on the fence in the corner, the wild barrage of stalky, umbrella-shaped weeds in the stippled shade. He offered Jo and me four cents for every weed when the going rate was three, because he knew we were thorough. (You must dig a weed out at its base, work your trowel carefully through the dirt so you can scoop the whole thing out, with its roots intact. Most of the other weeders would give up halfway down and just yank out what they could. Weeds will almost always grow back in this soil, no matter what you do, but they take longer if you attack them at their roots.) Charlotte liked teasing us about it off and on, or rather, she liked teasing me, and if it weren't for Jo's reminding me each time that Charlotte was just speaking out of envy, I may have minded more than I did.

And I did mind, but not enough to stop hanging around with her. I put this information down so you'll know our history with Charlotte and how it was to be friends with her, so you won't be surprised when I tell you that Jo and I hadn't spoken with her (except at school) since our afternoon in the cemetery, nor with Phillipa and Fay, until they stopped by Mr. Dharma's garden the following week.

Anyone willing to talk about that Friday will probably want to tell you about Auntie Coco's sister and how she disappeared that night, never to be found. One or two of our neighbors might even share with you some gossip, if you're patient enough to get them going, if you can wait without interfering for subtle disclosures to be made in the midst of aimlessly unwinding sentences, for secrets to be unmasked in glances cast askance, for the sudden lowering of a tone, the last spoken word precious as a gem. Jo and I weren't home that night, and there's no point to my piecing together for you what we weren't around to witness when I could tell you about the afternoon, instead, irrelevant as some of it may be to what you think you want to know . . .

We, too, were once like you.

LULU MENDEZ

M ADAM NEVER EXPLAINED to Malika why suddenly
she was afraid of burglars entering the house while they
were asleep. And Malika hadn't asked about it because the truth
was that she had never been comfortable sleeping with the windows open all night. She used to worry especially about the
children, even though Malika herself was only twelve when
Madam's mother had sent her down from Malacca to help out.
(Malika, like both Madam and Sali, was Malaccan by birth, and
from what I've heard, Malika's mother had taken care of Madam
when Madam was a child, and it was she who had suggested to
Madam's mother that Malika be sent over when Madam became

pregnant with Caroline. Madam's main help at the time was a Sri Lankan woman already in her fifties, whom Madam's mother-in-law had hired for Madam and her husband when they got married, and who no doubt was having her hands full with Francesca, who had been two at the time. That was what Malika's mother had argued, or so Malika would recall the conversation that had taken place on the other side of a closed bedroom door a few afternoons before she was put on the small, crowded bus to Singapore. On that bus Malika had stared through the dusty, half-open window at the passing rows of rubber trees, while the bodies of the other passengers surged and hurled themselves back and forth around her. She had had to stand, even though Madam's mother had paid for a seat, because a skinny twelve-year-old girl had to rely on the kindness of strangers, and on the occasion that the kindness was missing, that was simply one's fate for the day. And so she had stood, her insides twisted in a hard, tight ache, unbearable at first, only by the time the bus was pulling into the terminus on this side of the Causeway, miles of dust and sweat (hers and that of strangers leaning much too close for her liking) were clinging to her like a sick rash, and Malika's relief when she recognized Madam waving to her on the pavement outside, with Ahmad, the chauffeur, waiting patiently by Madam's side to carry Malika's bag for her, was so great, it felt to Malika like a burst of joy, and the ache from hours ago became nothing more than a simple throbbing, nothing more than another heartbeat whispering against her ribs. She would forget it, not notice it for years, until after Michelle left. Only then would Malika start dreaming of the green gossamer light of the rubber trees. Only then would she wonder how anyone could misplace a memory of love.)

Malika's room was outside the kitchen, separated from the main part of the house by the passageway in which sat the washing machine and the dryer. It was a bigger room than either Sali's or mine, and Malika had had it to herself for years, since she was twenty-two (when the Sri Lankan woman had fallen ill with diabetes, and in spite of the fact that there were better doctors in Singapore and Madam had offered to pay for her medical expenses, Aatha, as she was called, had decided it was time to go home and live out her old age with her family). Even with the double bed (I, too, had a double bed in my room, but Sali's room had only a single bed), the armoire with a full-length mirror on one of its doors (Sali and I had only chests of drawers with mirrors on top), and a small blue desk that had once been shared between Francesca and Caroline when they were in primary school (by the time Michelle came along, Madam's husband's insurance firm was doing so well, he and Madam had decided to renovate the house and buy all new furniture), even with all of that, there was enough floor space on which to set up Malika's Scrabble board if we so wished, or rather, when Sali could be cajoled into playing. (I enjoyed playing Scrabble very much and so, too, did Malika. Sometimes she would play with Madam's grandchildren when they visited, just as she had played with the girls when they were young. But the grandchildren owned a fancy deluxe edition, with a rotating base and a plastic board with a grid to prevent the tiles from sliding about. That was how Malika had come to inherit the old edition, which she kept in a corner of the blue desk, and which she much preferred because of its sentimental value.)

Of course in the beginning Malika had hoped for a different room eventually. Even the sewing room would have suited her, as small as it was and with a window facing part of the brick wall built by Madam's British neighbor around his house next door. (This was the neighbor living in the house to the right of Madam's when one looked at the houses from the road. He was a tall, reserved gentleman who as far as Malika knew worked for the British High Commission, and whom she would later nickname Prince Phillip because of the uncanny resemblance she thought he bore to the Queen's husband, but as Sali and I were never around when the neighbor stepped out of his house, we couldn't agree or disagree). Malika's heart had sunk when Aatha had left and she had realized the impossibility of finding a plausible enough excuse to ask for a room inside the house. Unveiling to Madam (who was still her employer, no matter how kind Madam was, and who would have had to consult her husband) either of her actual reasons was out of the question. And so the passing years had layered upon Malika's lips a silence shifting as the rubber leaves used to shift on the grounds of a plantation, in small spirals of resignation and a tapering hope. We could hear the inaudible sighs when she talked, or rather, we could feel their outline, like the glimmering impression hanging behind one's closed eyelids of things not there. Sali was too young and self-absorbed to be concerned, and perhaps so was I, but on occasion I would wonder if Malika had changed her mind after all, if she had come to her senses, as I saw it, and realized that few servants were as well off as she.

The sewing room was no longer used as a sewing room and, in fact, had been used only briefly when Madam had converted it into a sewing room in 1963 (Madam's school principal had assigned her to teach some of the sewing classes that year while the regular sewing teacher went on maternity leave, and Madam had confessed to Malika she was out of practice and that was why she needed Malika and Aatha to clear out the storeroom and clean it up, the sooner the better because Madam had purchased a new Singer and it was to be delivered within the week, one that even stitched buttonholes).

Another bird flew past one of Madam's windows on that Friday afternoon, the one in the sewing room this time. I was passing by the doorway on my way back from the bathroom. Sali had played enough with Madam's jewelry for the time being, and she and Malika had gone into Malika's room because Malika's room was cooler than Madam's without air conditioning. (Malika had an air conditioner in her room, which neither Sali nor I had, but during the day she preferred fresh air, since at night, her windows were always shut. I would have chosen air conditioning at any time, and Sali would have, too, if we could have chosen. It was only Malika who could afford to enjoy the shady, dappled light of the flamboyant trees outside her windows, enjoy the scratchy harmony of a breeze now and then rocking the leaves.) I felt the bird's shadow swerve over the sunlight just like before, and then there was only sunlight, hard and brilliant on the British gentleman's brick wall.

Malika was kneeling on the floor by the bed, unfolding the Scrabble board (the old edition had a cardboard one that folded in half for storage) and saying to Sali, "At some point, you should try not using the dictionary and see what happens," when I reached her room.

It was after four o'clock. A neighbor's servant (not the British gentleman's) was outside beating on a carpet, the flat slaps thudding away as the fence over which the carpet hung rattled beneath its weight. Otherwise the air was quiet, with not even the thread of a wailing baby anywhere.

Malika set the board down, then settled herself nimbly into a position in which she was sitting with her back against the bed. She stretched out her legs and swung them to the left of the board, and then she stared for a moment at her feet peeking out from her white salwar. She had always found her feet unfeminine, flattish-looking like a duck's feet, as she put it. Then she sighed and almost smiled, secretly, as if to remind herself to feel gratitude for small blessings bestowed on her by fate. A continued delay in the onset of arthritis was more than a small blessing of course, but Malika, like the rest of us, would realize this only in hindsight, only when the first tiny degree of a hint that flexibility was draining out of her limbs startled her, when she found herself wincing as she swung her legs over the side of the bed (such a simple action) on a morning yet to come.

But that time waited unforeseeably in the future on this afternoon, and except for Malika's news of her sighting of the girl behind the sugar cane, it seemed a Friday like any other. Sali and

I would stay until Madam came home, and then we would say hello to Madam and leave and return on the bus to our lives in Miss Shakilah's neighborhood (Sali worked for the Albuquerque family, and I, for Miss Dorothy Neo, who was a spinster). Although at the moment that I entered Malika's room a sensation of lightheadedness took hold of me and the room spun into a giddy whiteness, it was for no more than a few seconds. I blinked, and there was Sali standing by a window, gazing rather wanly at the flamboyant trees, and Malika was drawing columns on a foolscap pad in her lap.

"Birds seem to be circling all around the house today," I said, and Malika glanced up to see if I was referring in some way to the girl. When she saw I wasn't trying to, she turned her attention back to the columns, writing her name in neat, cursive blue letters at the top of the first one.

Sali continued to gaze out the window.

"I just saw another one zooming by the sewing-room window," I went on, sitting down on the floor beside the Scrabble board.

"No birds zooming by here," said Sali, and she heaved a sigh. Sometimes it all became too much for her, the languid breeze and the shadows of the flamboyant leaves hardly moving on the ground, the air watery, tepid with light. Even the tiled roof of Madam's next-door neighbor on this side and the flat white wall of the neighbor's house, partially visible through the banana trees along the fence, were so familiar as to depress her at times.

Malika was writing my name in the second column (always going by age), looping together the *l, u, l, u,* so gracefully like a repeated pattern in lace. (Sometimes I wondered which nun's handwriting it was that Malika had, only because I knew that before coming to Singapore, she had received some schooling in a convent.)

"When an ancestral spirit returns, it may take the form of a bird, you know," I said, mostly for Sali's sake. (Because of her poor reading habit, Sali knew very little about the world and wasn't even aware there were limits to her knowledge.)

She turned around with some interest. I watched her gaze flicker over Malika's bent head before she asked me if I was sure. I told her of course I was, and Sali looked at Malika again. But Malika didn't look up until she was done writing all our names, and then all she said was, "You want to try not using the dictionary today?"

"No way, okay?" said Sali. She came away from the window and sat down, folding her legs Buddha style, and shook her head as she faced Malika across the board. "What, let you both hantam me? No way."

Malika smiled and pulled her Oxford Dictionary out from under the bed where she kept it (so that it was within her reach if she needed to look up a word while she was reading at night). It was one of the few possessions she hadn't inherited from anyone, a Christmas present from Madam years ago, and Malika quite cherished it. The dictionary's spine had been loosened by her frequent use in the past, and the paper jacket had long been removed (Michelle had torn it accidentally one day when she was just over ten months old). Malika ran her fingertips gently over the navy-blue cover, before pushing the dictionary over to Sali.

Outside, the servant beating on the carpet continued to swing her woven bamboo bat at it, the sounds coming more slowly across the still air as her arm grew tired.

Sali reached into the maroon Scrabble bag and drew an X. "You see my luck-lah," she said, making a face. "That's why I don't like this game."

Malika chuckled as I reached in after Sali and drew an M. Then it was Malika's turn, and she drew an A, to which Sali reacted by rolling her eyes in an exaggerated show of mock displeasure. Her boredom with Singapore (a small-fry country with small-fry men, as Sali saw it) was subsiding, as was her impatience with her present life (laden with a lack of opportunity for chance encounters with Westerners, among whom her Hollywood film director was waiting, keeping an eye out for the exotic girl of his dreams). Sali was always happy for a spell during our afternoons at Madam's house. I watched as she dropped her X back into the bag. Then she leaned forward, balancing her elbows on her knees, and prepared to concentrate.

MALIKA WOULD NEVER manage to unearth what lay at the root of her anxiety about the children in the years that the family used to go to sleep with the windows open. (Even during the riots early in the 1970s, a few windows had been left ajar, Madam's husband insisting that as the fighting was between the Malays and the Chinese, being Eurasian, they were safe—he would not give in to intimidation by those lower-class hooligans, Malika would remember his saying to Madam one night when Madam had followed him into the bathroom and shut the door so they could speak privately). Nowadays she thought perhaps her imagination had simply been stirred by books, those fantastic volumes of foreign intrigue and romance Madam had shown her in the National Library and in which Malika would immerse herself night after night (it was Madam who had come up with the idea that Malika should apply for a library card, with which one was able to borrow four books at a time and keep them for two whole weeks).

Aatha hadn't shared Malika's concern about the windows, or so she had replied when after Michelle was born, Malika had inquired, timidly, if they would be able to hear the children cry out while the air conditioner was on. (She knew by then that she and Aatha wouldn't hear a thing above the drone of the air conditioner. In the first year of Caroline's birth, it was Aatha who had moved into the baby's room and slept there at night. And Malika, who had stayed in the room outside the kitchen, had listened until she realized she couldn't catch a single sound if it came from inside the house.)

Of course her anxiety had lessened when Madam finally reached her senses, especially now with just the two of them living in the house. (The truth was that Madam's decision to start closing the windows had come about not long after she had walked into the kitchen on an afternoon that Sali and I were sitting there, wondering out loud if the man who had raped Malika's friend thirty-one years ago was still alive. The fellow had never been caught and it was clear he wasn't going to be caught, given how much time had passed. Malika had been in the bathroom when Madam entered the kitchen, and later, when we suggested to her that Madam's decision may have resulted from her overhearing our conversation, Malika responded only that what had happened to Bettina wasn't news to Madam (Bettina had been a close friend of Malika's and perhaps for that reason, Malika could not bring herself to admit Bettina had been raped, although she did know about the baby, a stillbirth). I couldn't understand at the time her unwillingness to face the fact that as Madam was getting on in age and feeling less immortal, any memory of tragedy was bound to take on a new significance. But out of respect, Sali and I were leaving the topic alone.)

One would have to wonder if, in fact, Madam had known about the ghost in her garden, whether burglars, or rapists, weren't what she was worried about after all. What some of us would have to ask ourselves shortly (it was early on that Friday night that one of Miss Shakilah's neighbors would disappear, the sister of a woman known even to the other Madams as Auntie Coco, and given that she would never be found and what else was about to happen) and the question Malika would not be able to answer, no matter how often in the years to come she would sieve patiently through the afternoons and nights and mornings of her past living with Madam, was whether the girl behind the sugar cane was related to Miss Shakilah (perhaps an ancestor of hers who had died young), or whether Miss Shakilah, like Malika, had been chosen to be an instrument of some sort (in which case the girl may have appeared to Madam too, long before Miss Shakilah's visit).

It was Sali who asked out of the blue, in the middle of the game while Malika was pondering X-R-A-Y (worth thirty points because of the double-word score waiting beneath R-U-S-E) and E-X-I-L-E (worth twelve points, nothing extra, but it was a more exciting word), "What do you think she wants?"

Malika stroked her red bead with her right thumb (as was her habit when she was confronted with a dilemma). Without looking up from her row of letters, she replied, "I'm not sure. Sometimes all a ghost wants is prayer. But if that's so, poor thing. She's come to the wrong person, ya?"

"That can't be it," said Sali. "Ghosts usually know about people, right? From what I've heard, they seldom choose the wrong ones to appear to." She looked at me to see if I would confirm this piece of information, since Malika was engrossed with her choices of words at the moment.

"I thought you didn't believe the girl could be a ghost," I said.

"No, you're the one who doesn't believe she could be a ghost." Sali waggled her finger at me as if chiding a naughty child. She smiled when she saw I was annoyed, and I had to stop myself from falling into one of our habitual tussles. (Sometimes she took our friendship too far. Given the difference in our ages, had we been sisters, she would have had to show me some of the respect she showed Malika, and that we were unrelated was no excuse, as I saw it. But Sali's teasing was only a displacement of her daily frustration with life. That was the reason I put up with it.)

A rustle in the flamboyant trees caught Malika's attention. Her thumb and finger squeezing the red bead, she stared past Sali's head, in the direction of the sprays of scarlet flowers and pinnate leaves and bright sky. Sali, too, found herself turning around, her lips parted slightly in anticipation of a glimpse of the supernatural (as if anyone could see it simply by desiring to).

But it was only an afternoon breeze, passing more restlessly than usual over the branches of the flamboyant trees, shaking the air as if it were full of seeds.

Sali caught her reflection in the mirror on the door of the armoire as she turned back to the game. Wisps of hair hung stickily about her face, stringy as seaweed in the damp heat, and she was about to smile and gesture to herself when she saw me rolling my eyes in the mirror. She swung around.

"What?" she said sharply. "Why you always want to make fun of me? You don't have any wishes of your own, is it?"

"You're letting the heat fry your brain," I said, as I didn't think there were grounds for her accusation. (It was true that I hadn't chosen to entertain Sali's daydreams with Malika's patience, but I didn't make fun of them regularly as she was implying. Indeed, what I usually did was to remain silent and uninvolved.)

"Aiya, you two," murmured Malika. She let go of her bead, picked up her chips, leaned over the board and spelled E-X-I-L-E downwards, through the I of T-R-I-E-D like a sword and onto the tail of P-L-A-N which then was P-L-A-N-E, a sum total of nineteen points.

We weren't surprised to find out later (when I won) about the thirty points Malika had sacrificed. Malika always went for the more interesting word in the end, the more musical word or the word cloaked in degrees of interpretation, as if she were addicted or in love, and couldn't resist or say no once a word had caught her fancy. (X-R-A-Y, she would point out, was dull, dull because of its lackluster vowel and dull because it evoked only illness, particularly consumption.)

It was around a quarter past six when we heard the long, slow swing of the wrought-iron gate, and then the gentle purr of Madam's silver-gray Corolla as it pulled into the driveway and came to a stop under the aluminum roof of the car porch, in front of the sugar cane.

The car door opened and closed, a thump dropping into the evening air like an overly ripened fruit. It was followed (as always now) by the closing swing of the gate, and after that, Madam's voice was singing through the walls of the house, calling out for Malika as we were putting away the Scrabble board and as the flamboyant trees began to grow noisy, shrill with the prattle of mynah birds.

"Any messages?" Madam wanted to know, after all of our hello's, and Malika was about to tell her Mrs. Allen (a family friend) had called in the morning to invite Madam over for lunch on Sunday and the upholsterer had called at noon to say the dining-room chairs were ready for delivery, when Madam asked first, "Did Miss Shakilah call?"

"No, Madam, Miss Shakilah didn't call," said Malika, almost apologetically as if it were her fault somehow. (She hadn't known Miss Shakilah was supposed to call, but it was apparent from Madam's tone a call had been expected.)

Madam gave a small sigh, and as Sali and I were leaving we heard her asking if Caroline had called. (Caroline was the one who called home most regularly, much to Madam's and Malika's surprise. Her calls came once a week at least, sometimes two, three times, usually in the morning, after the boys were in their beds in Vancouver, Canada.) We didn't hear Malika's answer.

Perhaps it was a yes and Madam had smiled, and Malika had smiled back conspiratorially, her heart swollen with a bittersweet understanding.

All one could hear walking away around the side of the house at that hour was the searing cry of the mynah birds, sharp and thick as it billowed over the flamboyant trees.

MADAM WENT OUT again after dinner (boiled rice with fish curry that Madam had brought home for her and Malika, and the sambal kangkung that Malika had fried up in a matter of minutes). Malika was in the kitchen, draping the white dish towels over their red plastic hooks on the wall above the dish rack when she heard the Corolla leaving the driveway. She gazed out the window towards the light that was on in a room downstairs in the neighbor's house, where the soft gurgle of running water floated into the night behind the banana trees. (She no longer wondered if her nightmares had been brought on by the proximity between her room and the banana trees, since the trees were on the neighbor's side of the fence and beyond Madam's control to do anything about, or so Malika had rationalized each time she had decided not to tell Madam about the nightmares. Malika couldn't be sure what Aatha may have known or suspected. Aatha had never mentioned the nightmares or asked Malika whom it was she was wrestling and trying to push away in her sleep, and since Aatha herself had seemed to sleep peacefully, Malika had concluded after a while that the banana trees weren't haunted after all. Not all banana trees were, as she knew.) She turned from the window when the sound of the Corolla's engine had faded in the distance, evaporating like the trail of a Boeing 747 passing overhead.

It was half-past seven. (Later she would remember glancing at the kitchen clock, at the black numerals and the position of the two black hands on the round white face, there on the wall above the refrigerator. She had noted the hour by force of habit. Malika always knew when to expect Madam back when Madam went out, especially when Madam was taking one of her drives to the airport, as she had told Malika she was doing this evening. She knew then that Madam was unlikely to bump into a friend and be delayed spontaneously.)

Malika put the bowl of oranges and apples that sat on the kitchen table during the day back in the center of the table, a porcelain bowl hand-painted in coruscant swirls of azure and magenta, which Madam and her husband had found in a backstreet potter's shop in Macao ages ago, just after they were married and before Francesca was born. (Madam had been dismayed to discover the shop gone by the time she was in Macao again, in May of 1984, a year after her husband's passing. Madam was taking her first vacation alone that time, unaccompanied even by the children. The former back street had become a thoroughfare, developed almost beyond recognition, she would tell Malika upon her return. None of the other proprietors had been able to tell her where she might find the Portuguese potter she had met on her previous trip, and while Malika was unpacking Madam's suitcase and sorting through unworn clothes and clothes to be washed, Madam had speculated out loud that perhaps the potter had passed away, her voice filling with regret the way a well slowly fills with rain during the monsoon. Or so Malika would remember as she was looking back, on one of her mornings yet to come.)

She turned off the kitchen light after picking up the book she was in the middle of reading from her blue desk (switching on the lamp on the armoire before she left the room), and walked to the front of the house to settle herself in one of Madam's cane armchairs on the patio, a habit she had started forming after Michelle left, on those first few nights after the wedding, when the silence in the house had been deafening and Madam had started going out for her drives alone on the new highway.

From the patio one could catch the sounds of Madam's neighbors on the right (on the left if one was looking from the road), a family of four. One might hear the thud of an object dropping on the floor (slipping out of the hands of one of the children, Malika presumed—the son was four, the daughter was five), the clink of a glass or the tinnier ring of a metal utensil, and sometimes voices. Bits of parental conversation might ripple out of a window and drift through the thick hibiscus hedge along the fence, or the son's voice (more often than the daughter's) might break out, raised in a pouting protest. One could hear, too, if one were attentive enough, traffic humming on the main road a quarter of a mile away, a soothing slush of tires through puddles if there had been rain, or on a still night like tonight, just a whirring rhythm of the engines of different cars, the squealing crescendo of a bus approaching a stop, and in Madam's garden an almost imperceptible bristling of night insects beating about in the sultry air.

As on other nights, the British neighbor's house remained quiet, except for the occasional peal of the telephone, which if it rang would stop after two rings and then the answering machine would click on (or so Malika assumed, since that was what had happened once when Madam had had to call the gentleman because the postman had delivered to her by mistake a letter addressed to him). Malika couldn't tell as she opened her book (a French novel in English translation, about a love affair between a French teenage girl and a Chinese man in the time that Vietnam and Cambodia were known as Indochina) whether the gentleman was home or not, as his house was hidden from view by the brick wall. (It was a one-story bungalow, built in sprawling pavilion style like Madam's, whereas the other houses on the road were two-story and semi-detached, built on a smaller acreage each.)

The page on which Malika had stopped reading on the previous night (when she had read in bed as Madam had been home) was marked by a vermilion leather bookmark, fringed at one end and bearing a gilt sketch of a domed building (a souvenir from Vatican City, sent to Malika while Francesca was on one of her business trips in Rome). Malika was removing the bookmark when, out of the corner of her eye, she saw the sugar cane quiver, over there to her right, four feet or so from the edge of the car porch. She was about to turn her head when she caught herself. No need to scare the poor thing away, Malika told herself, as she placed the bookmark back on the page. She didn't close the book. She let her hand rest on the page, caressing the fringe on the bookmark with the tips of her fingers.

The sugar cane grew still. Malika waited for a message, for the girl to speak to her. (If the girl wanted prayer, she thought, she would do as Madam had done after her husband's passing and each time one of the children was getting married. She would write a petition on a slip of paper, fold it neatly, and leave it in the wooden box with a slot in the Church of St. Francis of Assisi, which wasn't far down the road, within walking distance. The box hung on a wall in the enclave in which dozens of votive candles burned daily on a tiered iron rack in front of the statue of the Blessed Virgin. Miracles were said to have happened for petitioners who had left their requests there, although of course not for every one of them. Malika couldn't think of a better solution, if what the girl's soul needed was prayer. Asking Madam if she could attend the Sunset Mass with her (as Malika had been invited to, several times in the past) was out of the question. As far as Malika knew, the lascivious Father Johnson was still there, since Madam would have mentioned it if Father Johnson had retired or been transferred to another parish, although not because Madam was aware the Father's hands had once slithered (seemingly by accident) over Malika's buttocks. Malika was sure Madam didn't know, not even when Francesca started attending Mass at the Novena Church instead, with Caroline and later Michelle tagging along.)

When no message seemed to be coming forth, Malika looked up and saw there was no longer anyone hiding in the sugar cane. But someone had been there. Malika would not be able to explain to Sali and me how she could be so sure it had been the same girl as on Wednesday but she was, even though one could hardly make anything out in the murky shadows at the garden's edge.

A light came on in an upstairs window above the hibiscus hedge, and someone moved behind the curtains. Next door to her left, Malika heard footsteps coming along the slate path in the British neighbor's garden. She listened as his gate opened, then closed, with a quick drop of the iron latch. The footsteps continued down the road. She tried to discern if they were a man's or a woman's, but all she could tell was that they weren't the British gentleman's. (She would have recognized his, having heard them on numerous occasions over the years.)

She leaned towards the doorway behind her and checked the clock on the living-room wall. It was five minutes past eight. Madam wasn't late in returning from her drive, not yet, so Malika couldn't explain the tingling in the pit of her stomach, her spidery sense of foreboding, unless it had somehow been brought on by the girl. But she wasn't afraid of the girl. Ghosts didn't frighten Malika simply by being ghosts. She was more afraid of wolves dressed up in the clothing of lambs.

She wondered what the girl might want from her if not prayer and, closing her book, sat back to wait.

SUSANNA WANG

ALPHONSUS WONG WASN'T Charlotte's first (and if he thought he was, he was a fool, as he and Charlotte weren't even going steady because Charlotte thought going steady would cramp her, make her feel claustrophobic, as she'd put it, but saying it to us, not to him). She was probably with him while Phillipa and Fay came looking for us, their shadows stretching past the yam and pandan leaves as they stepped in and out of the shade of the cemetery trees. (Phillipa had been the tallest and fastest girl in our class before Fay arrived, but they were on the track team together now, often running neck and neck at practice.) We didn't hear them approach Mr. Dharma's gate, but when Jo turned around to work on a straggly clump behind her, suddenly there they were.

As on other weekday afternoons, Mr. Dharma wasn't home because he was teaching in the afternoon session that year. (He used to teach history and geography at St. Peter's, which as you may know is still one of St. Agnes' brother schools.) All you had to do to let yourself into any of our neighbors' gardens was slip your arm through a dragon's mouth and slide the bolt back, since it wouldn't be until some years after Auntie Coco's sister's disappearance that people would start using padlocks. Jo and I had been working since two o'clock as usual, and when Phillipa and Fay found us, it was nearly half-past three. Some rain clouds were moving in from the beach and the air in Mr. Dharma's garden sagged with humidity, with diffused light and the fragrances of his rambutans and papayas, with the ochreous tincture of freshly dug earth, and of seaweed, but you could still feel the sun on your head as Jo was calling out, "Hey," to Phillipa and Fay, as Phillipa reached in with her right hand and lifted the latch and slid the bolt back.

They had come to ask us if we wanted to participate in Charlotte's deal with her cousin Leonard, who was a St. Peter's boy (as was Alphonsus Wong but for obvious reasons, Charlotte was leaving him out of the picture).

"We're proposing fifty-five cents for a nipple, but if a boy wants to see both nipples, we'll give him a discount. He can get two nipples for a dollar. Taking off our panties is more expensive. Three dollars or five dollars, depending on whether he wants us to squat for him." Phillipa paused so Jo and I could assess how we felt about the terms of the deal as she had stated them. Then she went on, very matter-of-factly, "If you want to charge more, better give Charlotte a call, okay? They're meeting to sign the agreement after the dang-ki's performance tomorrow."

"What dang-ki?" I asked.

"You don't know there's one going to be at the market

tomorrow?" Phillipa glanced sideways at Fay, and Fay nodded, her short hair bobbing in the sun, spiky as grass. (Fay wore her hair shorter than most boys did, but her haircut looked so surprisingly feminine with her elfin face, the nuns were leaving her alone about it.)

"I knew," said Jo, and she added when I looked at her, "I was going to tell you."

"They've already marked out the area," Phillipa went on. "He's going to be in front of the noodle stalls. There's a square drawn in red chalk on the cement."

"How big?" asked Jo.

"About ten feet by ten feet?" Phillipa looked again at Fay, who nodded again. "Ya, about that big."

Jo turned to me. "So if we can get a place right along the border of the square, we'll be able to see quite a lot. We should be there by three o'clock, at least half an hour early. Okay?"

There was no question that we were going, and no need for Jo to ask me if I wanted to go because she knew my heart, knew the rise and fall and twists of its passions as if they belonged to her own heart's churning. There was also no question that we would have to lie about going to watch a dang-ki, so if you were to ask our mothers, they would tell you Jo and I were at the cinema that Saturday, and I ask that you not let on to them what you know, or what else you may find out.

"Okay," I said to Jo, with all the boldness and naiveté of girls our age then.

She whipped out her old, sly smile, wheels turning in her head, and I saw instantly what she was thinking, but I wasn't about to bring it up in front of Phillipa and Fay.

"So what about Charlotte's deal with Leonard? Are you guys in or not?" asked Phillipa, returning to the topic because Charlotte needed our answer no later than that evening, in case Jo and I weren't interested and she and Phillipa had to round up some other girls.

I shrugged, and Jo replied that we would have to discuss it first. She didn't look at me as she was telling Phillipa this, but I knew she had caught the hesitation in my shrugging, and so had Fay, who was staring at Jo and me as if she hadn't noticed before how well we could read each other's body language.

Phillipa already knew how Jo and I were, so all she said was, "Okay, if you don't call Charlotte by seven o'clock tonight, we'll assume you're in, and that you agree with the fees I gave you. Right? Okay?"

"Right," said Jo, and I nodded, but then Jo added, "If we're in, we'll go over to Charlotte's house instead of phoning. I want to see what the agreement says before it gets signed." She shot me a quick glance. I said nothing.

"It says exactly what I've told you, but okay-lah, if you must see for yourself, go ahead. I'll let Charlotte know." Phillipa tossed her hair back as she turned to look at Mr. Dharma's front door. She had gorgeous wavy hair, and she watched the door as if she expected it to open, and Mr. Dharma to stand there and warn us in the manner of our teachers not to fall prey to the Devil, to the unchaste and morally improper thoughts the Devil was known to take great pleasure in sowing in teenagers. (Like Charlotte and several others, Phillipa had a bit of a crush on Mr. Dharma, who was quite a dreamboat back then. Fay seemed unaffected, however, as were Jo and I. He wasn't our type, if you must know.)

"So have you heard of anyone else seeing them?" Fay asked suddenly, her voice barely an echo, a wisp of thrumming over our heads.

Phillipa continued to watch Mr. Dharma's door, although she was listening. You could feel her listening.

I looked at Jo, who returned my look as she told Fay, "Not yet."

"Do you think other people will see them?" Fay went on.

"Sooner or later," said Jo, sounding so sure, I didn't doubt that she was right.

"But so far, you haven't heard anyone talking about it, right?"

We knew Fay liked living in Singapore, liked being an only child in her uncle's house, liked having a whole room and a bed to herself. (Phillipa had found out about Fay's eight younger siblings over in Jakarta, whom Fay always had to give way to so she could set them a good example. It had been Fay's uncle's idea for her to come and stay with him in Singapore, so she could concentrate on her studies. And so if Fay's parents were to hear of how he couldn't keep her out of trouble, she would most likely be hauled back at once. She wouldn't have been in the cemetery with us if Phillipa hadn't somehow talked her into it, and you could feel her starting to grow apprehensive towards their friendship.) Jo assured her none of our neighbors were talking about what we had seen, which meant the odds were in our favor that no one had seen us.

"You're sure, right?"

Phillipa turned to Fay then, and said, "Look, if someone knows we were there, we would be hearing about it by now, okay? Didn't I already tell you?"

Fay nodded, and gave us a halfhearted smile.

"You're not going to back out of this deal now, are you?" asked Phillipa.

Fay said no, she wasn't. She sighed, and I could feel Jo was starting to feel sorry for her (because beneath the tough tomboy exterior you might hear about from the nuns if you were to speak to them, Jo was kind, and her heart could melt faster than butter on an open flame). So I knew the die was cast. For Fay's sake, Jo wouldn't back out, either, and that was why I was ready to say yes later when we were alone, after Phillipa and Fay were gone.

IT WAS AROUND half-past four that they left, and Auntie Helena had stepped out shortly after for her weekly gambling game with Father O'Hara and Sister Sylvia. (The three would gather every Friday night in the parish house, and you'd see them huddling over their cards at one end of the dining table, the ceiling fan whirring softly over their heads. They were supposed to be playing just for fun, but everyone knew there was money involved. People simply looked the other way because where was the harm in letting three senior citizens exchange their money among themselves? Sister Sylvia was the oldest, a firecracker of a nun in her time, but that's another story. By the time we knew her, she was already living at Holy Family, cooking and keeping house for the priests. We used to think she'd outlive even Auntie Helena, the youngest of the trio.)

Jo was starting to ask me if I was feeling shy about showing my body to a boy when we heard Auntie Helena opening her door next door. She may not have heard us, but she was home at the time, for whatever it's worth.

We exchanged hellos through the fence and then Jo and I watched her drive off in her car. I can't say I noticed anything unusual about Auntie Helena that afternoon, nothing that would point to what was about to happen to her, what she would see in the morning . . .

"ODD IN WHAT way?" I asked, when Jo said there was something odd about Auntie Helena when she was closing her gate. But she simply shook her head and repeated, "Odd," as she picked up her basket of weeds and carried it over to Mr. Dharma's steps, her feet in sandals moving deftly through the grass like fish underwater as she crossed the garden.

"So anyway, is that why you don't want to do it? Are you feeling shy?" she asked me again.

I gathered the last of the stalks I'd dug up and stood up with my basket. "What if they want to touch?" I asked, walking over to join her at the steps.

"Dummy, that's why I want to see the agreement. We can make sure it says no touching."

"But what if they insist? Who's going to stop them? Each of us will be alone by then, right?"

"No, we'll go off two at a time. Two girls with two boys at a time. All you have to do is go behind some trees for privacy. You don't have to go far. The rest of us will wait and if a boy breaks the agreement, all you have to do is yell, and everything will come to a halt. The whole agreement will be off. We'll make sure Leonard knows that."

"What if Charlotte doesn't agree?"

"She'll agree. She needs us."

And that was all the discussion there was about Charlotte's plan.

YOU DON'T NEED to know whether we really went through with it. That, too, is another story. What matters is that you see who we were, see what was in our hearts that August, our very ordinary hearts.

You'll hear her story beckoning in the cemetery if you try. Stand where we were and let her face brush yours, the unfinished mask of her face hanging like wind off the branches, threading a way through the coarse grass and among the gravesites, whistling low in the lalang that used to grow deeper in.

You could see it in Jo's face that she was going to ask the dang-ki to show us who the diamond woman was. (We had sworn off the bomoh because she seemed too dangerous, but the dang-ki was a medium of a different caliber. As his powers were temporary, available to him only after a seven-day stint of fasting and meditation, he seemed to us less aligned with the spirit world, and so less of a risk. But then, all we had ever done before was watch, and I wouldn't have thought to ask for his help. I wouldn't have dared, without Jo.)

She wouldn't have done it, if I had stopped her. I could have stopped her. You should know this about us, how we wouldn't have forced each other into anything. But I wanted to see it, to watch the dang-ki sketch the diamond woman's features while he was in a trance, mark the curve of her chin on one of his thick, yellow squares of spirit paper . . .

Jo was sure we had saved enough to pay him in full.

So when Saturday afternoon came around, I emptied my share of our earnings onto my bed. I wrapped a rubber band around the dollar notes and picked up the loose change.

Jo was leaning on the gate when I stepped out of the house, her money pinned safely to the inside pocket of her yellow knapsack, not in a purse which could get snatched. She grinned when she saw me with my knapsack, too.

We were two foolish tycoons, about to embark on an adventure with no inkling of the cost. We didn't even wonder if perhaps we weren't the first ever to ask a dang-ki about the diamond woman.

I watched Jo slide the ribbon off her ponytail before we started walking. She seldom wore her hair loose but when she did, it was wavier and more gorgeous than Phillipa's, with a soft black sheen like moonlight over water, and the power to get us just about anything we desired.

"Ready?" she asked.

I said yes.

ROSE SIM

I REMEMBER HIS hair, blond like James Dean's, with the sun filtering through the bougainvillea outside the windows to our left lighting up the tips over his forehead. For some reason, I wanted to touch it, the fellow's hair, which to this day I don't know if I can explain, but there you have it. Maybe that's why it's always the first thing I remember about the afternoon, Chandra's boyfriend's hair, because up close, I could see that not only was it blond, but also feathery. Like a yellow canary's feathers accidentally doused in Clorox, I was thinking, and not like hair at all.

It was almost two o'clock, and Auntie Coco's sister was still with her. That's the other thing I think about, whenever I look back, how my shift at the library went till three on Fridays, and that Friday, Shak and I had already made plans for me to go over to her house after work.

Mundane facts, all mixed in with everything else.

By eight o'clock that night, Auntie Coco's sister would be missing, and Auntie Coco would start wandering up and down the road, dressed in her sarong and calling for her sister, her voice carrying so much anguish, it would spin and somersault over our rooftops and into the cemetery trees like a piece of her actual heart, and Shak and I would not be able to look at each other as we walked over to the door to look out. (We would be in the living room when it happened. Shak's mother was making mutton curry for dinner, I remember, and she had invited me to stay and eat. Mutton curry used to be one of our favorite dishes, you know, Shak's and mine. Our favorite hawker was the one who used to sell outside the convent, some fellow who always wore a coolie hat and no shirt. You could get from him one enormous bowl for fifty cents, which Shak and I would share because neither of us could finish the bowl by ourselves, but it was cheaper than buying two small bowls.)

About Chandra's boyfriend, there was nothing unusual about his being at the library that afternoon, since part of Chandra's reason for dating angmos was to show off. What was unusual was his coming over to talk to me, standing so close now that I could see, for the first time, what angmo hair was like, downy like an animal's. It would be like touching an animal, I thought, while he was introducing himself. Like gently stroking the breast of a canary, a bird so used to living in the cage, if it were to be set free in the morning, by sunset it would be dead.

That's what I've heard, about the canary.

"Jason Hill." He had stretched out his hand, so what was there for me to do but shake it?

So I shook his hand, his palm fleshy and heavy and slightly sweaty.

Since this fellow was the first foreigner ever to come up and introduce himself to me, I was a bit wary, wondering what he wanted. Usually, foreigners went for other types, right? Not someone like me. I wasn't sexy enough for most of them, and definitely not pretty enough. Even those who came here to the East, as they put it, hunting for a Chinese wife, even they passed me up. Those ex-army types. Foreigners all wanted someone who looked like Shak, or Serena Chan (who, by the way, had bought the house next-door to Ivan Anthony a few years after we were out of school, and now the two of them had something hot and secret going on, which all the neighbors knew about), or Isabella, if Isabella weren't a Sister. This was how they were, the angmos. Not so different from Chinese men, the traditional kind. Even if, mostly, they were looking for wives to stay barefoot and pregnant, as Shak used to say, when she was in her feminist mood, even so, the wives must be sexy. Or pretty. At least one or the other.

I don't remember how he got around to it, the fellow. One minute he was telling me his name and saying, "You're Rose Sim, aren't you?" and shaking my hand, while I looked past him to where some teenagers were coming into the library, four or five of them piling in through the revolving door and almost getting stuck, and the next minute, he was asking me if it was true there was a baby ghost following Shak around.

His exact words were, "Is it true your friend's being followed by a baby ghost, the woman who lives in America? Shakilah. Did I say her name right?"

He hadn't said it right, so I pronounced it for him, and he tried to imitate me, but his accent seemed to get in the way. Still, it was better than his first attempt, so I didn't correct him again.

Also, I didn't know what he was talking about. A baby ghost. Following Shak around? I knew at once it must have been Chandra who had passed the rumor on to him. But where had Chandra heard it? I was sure she hadn't started it herself, because I had never known her to have the imagination.

"Rose? Do you mind my asking you?"

More teenagers were coming into the library, and the revolving door kept swinging around in a zigzag pattern of sunlight and shadows.

We were near the bookshelves on the left side of that main floor, in the PN section. I remember because of the bougainvillea outside the windows, flourishing so bright pink against the glass. (The windows were closed because of the air conditioning, which was also why so many teenagers used our library, because not many of the smaller branch libraries were airconditioned in those days.) I remember I had a cart with me, so I must have been reshelving books when this Jason fellow had come up and started talking to me. I could feel the metal handle against my fingers, and I could see, when the revolving door slowed down, outside the air was moist, the heat shimmering over the cement steps and the sago palms at the edge of the library garden.

Sometimes the evocation of a spirit is enough to bring it near, you know, but there was nothing. I saw and felt nothing. So I asked this Jason fellow why he wanted to know about the baby ghost.

"You have a lot of ghost stories," he said. He smiled, his eyes bluer than the sea, I noticed. "You Singaporeans, I mean. You tell a lot of ghost stories. Every Singaporean has a ghost story in the family closet. Isn't that so, Rose?"

"Singapore has a lot of ghosts," I said, smiling so he would think I was joking.

Angmos never know how to understand ghosts, you know, calling everything superstition even in the face of eyewitness accounts. This one, for instance. Even after hearing enough stories, and for sure, not all from Chandra, the fellow wasn't interested in the truth, I could tell. Because he was assuming there was no truth. Otherwise, he would have done some background checking already, to find out more about our history, not only the parts everyone knows (about the Europeans coming and taking over the spice trade, and all that), but also the earlier parts. At least if he knew enough to think about Srivijaya and Majapahit, he could figure out for himself how as long ago as that, people here were cutting deals with the spirits. (The women, of course. Signing contracts by fasting and not combing their hair, letting themselves look ugly and mad, all for the sake of their husbands and sons, or sometimes, to protect their fathers. Because there was so much fighting and killing, how else could those empires have been built?)

Ghosts were roaming the region centuries before this fellow's ancestors arrived, and here he was, talking about them as if they were just a figment of our imagination.

All he wanted was fodder for his letters home, so he could write interesting things about his life here, to his buddies or his family or maybe even a girlfriend who was foolishly waiting for him to return, having no idea he was over here sowing his wild oats with Chandra. That's how foreigners are, the angmo ones who come here. Using our own stories against us, to prove that in spite of our commercial success, we're still a backward people. Still believing in ghosts. (Ask me whether I would bet my soul that by telling our stories, the foreigner thinks he can sound interesting to other people. As long as he doesn't say he believes in the stories, he feels safe talking, right?)

So I wasn't going to give this Jason fellow any information, even if I had some, which I didn't. I wasn't sure why Chandra had bothered to tell him about the rumor in the first place, unless it was to pantang Shak, bring her bad luck, that sort of thing. To make certain Shak couldn't use her charm to lure away her boyfriend, in case they happened to meet. I could imagine Chandra thinking up such a plot, because she was that sort. To her, what we all wanted was a blondie boyfriend.

If so, why pantang someone like that, right? And not only Shak but her baby as well, saying there was a ghost following them around.

I was getting angry, thinking about it. And maybe that Jason could sense there was no point talking to me further, because he didn't ask any more questions.

SO WHEN SHE showed up, Chandra, on the dot at two o'clock, I glared at her with as much disapproval as I could muster. I would have fired her off if we were by ourselves, but I didn't want her to lose face in front of an angmo, whether he was her boyfriend or not. Call me prejudiced, but an angmo's an angmo, I thought. Even if Chandra ended up marrying this one, and every soul is supposed to be sacred, I couldn't help feeling a gap between their kind of people and our kind of people, you know. Maybe because of Singapore's history with Europeans, or maybe the gap's always been there, it didn't matter to me as I looked at her, Chandra. What mattered was, I kept cool, so to speak. I simply glared at her, and when she said, "Hi, Rose," I could hear in her voice, she had gotten the message.

And when she didn't ask what her boyfriend and I had been talking about, now that she knew, I thought to myself, mission accomplished. Making Chandra feel uncomfortable gave me a lot of satisfaction, I must admit. Partly because I was tired of watching her walk into the library with her short skirts, carrying her high heels in her Gucci bag so she could put them on afterwards when her angmo boyfriend picked her up. She was wearing them now, the high heels, and a black skirt so tight, you had to wonder how her hips could get enough oxygen to sway so hard from side to side as she walked. I had heard her approaching us, of course, clickety clack all the way across the floor. And even though I hadn't turned around, I knew how Chandra walked, and also, Jason's eyes had confirmed it. The look he had given her. If he were a dog, his tongue would have been hanging out already.

"How's Shak?" she asked, finally.

"She's fine," I said, very politely on purpose.

"I hear she's due in December."

"Yes."

"How is she coping with the heat?"

"Getting used to it." Only a white lie, right? "This is her home, you know."

"Well, they say the blood gets altered after you've lived overseas." Chandra smiled at Jason, in such a way that she was almost batting her eyelashes, for no reason except to be alluring. He hadn't said anything, and she wasn't even talking directly to him.

If Shak's boyfriend had come home with her, she would never have behaved that way, I thought, and I was certain. Especially not in front of me, because it was rude to do this, like almost making love in public.

But that was how Chandra was. Sometimes I couldn't stand the sight of her. Otherwise, live and let live, as even the Mother Superior would say.

I was trying not to watch Chandra and her boyfriend as they left the library, their hips bumping like magnets. Because it was what she wanted, to draw attention to herself. So I turned to the windows and tried to wipe the picture of them out of my mind, the two of them pulok-pulok as if long-lost lovers, while I stared at the bougainvillea, at the hot sky, at the yellow library wall, at the black hair of teenagers leaning glumly with their elbows on the long table near the windows, studying. (Younger children also used our library, but their reading section was upstairs.)

A hand tapped me on the shoulder, and before I turned around, I knew who it was, because her scent had been there from the moment Chandra and her boyfriend had started walking away, that scent of her habit, of her hair, shorter now, rolled up like an old-fashioned Chinese scroll underneath her wimple. A whiff of the dampness in her armpits, making dewdrops on her skin.

She had waited until they left, I realized, and I wondered how I could have missed seeing her come over.

Isabella, whom Shak had already asked me about, because Shak didn't know, and how could she? Being away fifteen years and not even replying to my earlier letters with a postcard (which was why I had stopped writing to her, to Shak, because my feelings were hurt, although what I had told myself out loud was to be frugal and not waste stamps).

"Long time no see." Isabella was smiling such a wide smile, as if truly, from the bottom of her heart, she was happy to see me.

As I've said, I had been avoiding people from the past, so I hadn't stepped foot in the convent in years, you know. And as Isabella usually used the main library on Stamford Road when she was doing research for her teaching, she was easy to avoid, although I used to daydream sometimes that for some reason, she might come to use our library.

Now here she was, and I suspected I knew why.

Outside the revolving door, Chandra and her boyfriend were kissing, his pale hands holding her waist, not grabbing or fondling but so gentlemanly. He was like a Hollywood boyfriend in a black-and-white classic film, but I could tell from the way he wasn't letting go of her, their tongues were smacking inside their mouths. And also from the way some teenagers leaving the library were averting their eyes, because even they were embarrassed at such lack of self-restraint.

I wanted Isabella to know I also was glad to see her, but when I echoed her words, "Long time no see," they toppled out like tin cans, empty and false.

She pretended not to notice, just went on smiling before she started asking about Shak.

What surprised me was when she mentioned the baby ghost, only that wasn't how Isabella spoke of it. She called the ghost "the girl," and the way she eased into the topic, so matter-of-factly, I knew she couldn't have heard it from Chandra, but from someone reliable, someone she knew to believe, although I've never found out whom.

She didn't say the ghost was following Shak around, but rather, that Shak may be following a ghost. And she didn't say for sure, but maybe.

Mostly Isabella just wanted me to know, so I could be on the lookout. "You know our Shak. Make sure she doesn't do anything risky, Rose." She herself would be seeing Shak soon, but she wasn't going to bring up the girl if Shak didn't do it first.

So that's why, when I went over to Shak's house after work, and Shak told me she wanted to see the doctor's house, I would wonder if the baby ghost was involved. The girl, as Isabella put it. But I wouldn't be able to come up with a reason for us not to go.

And it may have had nothing to do with a ghost, you know. Nothing at all.

ACCOUNTS OF THE
FOLLOWING
SATURDAY IN

august 1994

HELENA SIM

daughter of koh siew lan (deceased)

father unknown

mother of rose

SISTER SYLVIA AND her winning hand. That was why-lah I
wasn't around when Auntie Coco started calling for her sister. Alamak, the luck that nun could have. And with her vow of
poverty, what was the point? Ah, so anyway, that was the reason I got home so late. Sister Sylvia and her winning hand. That
was it-lah. Every time she won, she wanted to play one more
round. She was already seventy-plus years old, how to say no to
her? Poor Father O'Hara, he wasn't young himself, you know.
By nine o'clock I could see him struggling to concentrate, his
eyelids already drooping. Both of us thought we were doing
penance-lah. Better here than in purgatory, ya? How could we

foresee that the old nun was nowhere near death, that actually she was going to live another ten years and Father O'Hara himself would go before her? Things like that, we can't know. Ah, so by the time I got home, all the commotion was over. Then, in the morning when I woke up, Rose was already out. No note to let me know what had happened or anything, everything like normal. That's my daughter for you. Saturdays she always worked half-day at the library, so I knew where she was. But anyone else's daughter would have left a short note—Mum, the police were here last night, Auntie Coco's sister got kidnapped, I'll tell you more later. Something like that, just for information. Not my Rose. She never liked excitement, okay? Always so quiet, from the time she was a child. Her father and I always knew, better not hope for grandchildren. How was our Rose going to find a husband, all the time her nose was buried in books? Both she and Valerie's daughter, although that one used to have all the boys trailing after her because she had the looks, what. Still, who ever expected Shakilah to come home like that? As if anyone was going to miss the fact that her finger was empty. But to be honest, I always liked her. At heart, she was a good girl. Always polite, always kind. And at least she knew how to get Rose to socialize a bit.

So anyway, Winifred Teo grabbed my arm that morning (we were at the char kway teow stall in the market, both of us happening to arrive there at the same time) and she began by asking me, in that busybody voice of hers, "Eh, Hel, did your daughter tell you what she told the police?"

You know Winifred. Forever paranoid, that woman. Alamak, as if she was so important, as if the government didn't have other things to worry about. She was wanting to compare notes, you see, in case different people had said different things to the police and the government became suspicious. That was how her mind worked. Of course, I didn't know right away what she wanted, thanks to Rose and her personality. So I had to ask, since

I couldn't ignore Winifred's mentioning the police. I thought at first, you know, something had happened to Rose. You know a mother's worst fears. And Rose being how she was, single like that, with no man in her life to protect her. Not even her father, anymore. Myself, I wasn't worried about, because who would want an old hag? But my Rose—she had beautiful skin, you know. So fair she was, like a swan. (She doesn't look the same nowadays, I don't know what happened, but before, she was just like a swan.)

So I asked Winifred, "What have you heard?"

That was how I managed to get her to give me the details, without her realizing that I didn't know anything. Otherwise, Winifred would have gone gossiping all over the neighborhood, about how Helena Sim's daughter didn't talk to her own mother and the two of them living in the same house, blah blah blah. I had to be very careful with her.

So, quietly, I let her talk, and of course, Winifred being herself, she was quite eager to do that. Luckily, I could control my facial expression while I was listening, so I managed to hide all the telltale signs of my true feelings, which were, first and foremost, relief that nothing had happened to Rose, and second, of course, I was confused like everybody else-lah, about who would want to kidnap the poor sister. She was mental, okay? Plus, she and Auntie Coco didn't seem to be rich. What I mean is this. They didn't look as though their family had money, ya? We always thought they were living off life insurance, something like that. Of course, everyone just assumed this. Auntie Coco was quite a hermit, so she never shared anything with us about her life, but we thought, probably she was married before, and then her husband must have died-lah.

What Winifred told me was this.

Babi! Babi! That was what everyone heard around eight o'clock the previous night, Auntie Coco's voice shouting for her sister outside on the road. Must have sounded a bit funny-lah.

You know what babi means in Malay. Pork! Pork! As if Auntie Coco was a hawker trying to get some business. Who knows how her sister had ended up with a nickname like that. Ya-lah, it must be short for Barbara but when you translated it, it still meant pork, okay?

So anyway, according to Winifred, Auntie Coco spoke only to Rose, Shakilah, and that boy Ivan when he went over to join them outside Valerie's gate (Rose was having dinner over there). Valerie herself hadn't stepped out, which wasn't surprising-lah. Poor thing, ya, losing face like that after she had spent all that money on her daughter's education. You know how expensive an overseas education can be, in America, especially. Ya-lah, Shakilah had become successful in her career, I'm not denying that, but her success wasn't enough to save the family's name, okay? If she had been a son, then of course, but she wasn't a son. Given people's mindset here, there's nothing more shameful than to have your daughter come home with a dumpling in the oven and no husband. Whether right or wrong, that was the situation, and it still is.

You know Winifred's friends with Teresa Albuquerque. (Birds of a feather-lah, those two, always boasting to each other about their sons, as if no one could tell that they were secretly competing over whether Adrian or Simon was getting more A's in each subject. At least I never did that to my Rose. I only told her, "Do your best," even though her results were never as good as Shakilah's. She's always been hardworking, you know, my Rose, but she never had Shakilah's brains, and luckily-lah. If she had wanted to go overseas for further studies, I don't know how I would have sent her.)

So anyway, Simon happened to be at Ivan's house at the time for extra maths tuition, so he knew it was Ivan who called the police. Must be because Auntie Coco herself was so distraught, poor thing.

"So, Hel, what did Rose tell them? They ask her the same

questions or not?" Winifred was asking me again, after she had finished spilling her news.

I pretended some more. "More or less the same." (They sounded like routine questions to me. When was the last time people had seen the sister, what was she wearing, that sort of thing, and also whether anyone had noticed any strangers lurking about recently.)

"More or less? What you mean, more or less?" See how gila she could be, that Winifred. Crazy woman.

"Wait-lah," I said, hoping for the best. "Let Rose tell you in her own words." I thought surely she would understand that, she who always wanted to be the first to tell people things herself.

She kept on trying. "Aiya, you can't tell me first?"

"No-lah, better not. You know my memory nowadays. I don't want to get the facts mixed up. Better you let Rose tell you."

"Aiya, okay-lah, okay-lah."

I was surprised. For Winifred, that was giving up a bit fast, okay? Then I noticed she was looking past me at Ying Ying Coleman, who was at that moment coming into the market, walking as usual two feet behind her husband as if this was China. If I didn't leave right away, Winifred was going to start jabbering about those two, and to be honest, any other day I wouldn't have minded chitchatting a bit. But I needed some time to absorb the news about Auntie Coco's sister. Plus, I was wondering what Rose herself knew, and also what Ivan had said to her, and what his manner had been-lah.

Not that I was harboring any false hope, okay? (Rose used to have such a crush on him, poor thing. She wouldn't admit it, but when she was a teenager, it was so clear she was pining for an impossible dream. Calling him Ivanhoe, of all things. You could see from an early age, that boy was going to grow up into a casanova. Look at him now, already thirty-plus and still swinging from girl to girl. That Serena should know better. Ah, and his poor parents, ya? They were in that TWA crash-lah, killed without the hope of any grandchildren. You see the problem when you're given a son who's too handsome for his own good.)

Anyway, it took some will power, but I told Winifred I better get on with my shopping. Alamak, you can't imagine how delicious the noodles smelled as I walked away. Garlic, sweet soya sauce, that aroma of fried cockles melting into the heat.

Supposedly that was when the old fellow had come through the gate after Ying Ying and her husband, and then followed them from stall to stall. Whether they themselves were aware of him or not, I don't know. And whether that old man had anything to do with what happened later, I don't know. As I was saying, I was too preoccupied with Winifred's news, because as you know, Singapore's so small, okay? People don't just disappear here.

That was where my mind was as I left the market (without finishing my shopping), and that's the truth. I don't know anything about the old fellow. (As for the girl, only now I'm hearing about that.)

WHAT I REMEMBER most clearly after that begins with the light. So bright the air became suddenly, blinding as frozen lightning, and it wasn't just my imagination, okay? The road shone like water as I was walking home, and people's fences and the leaves in the trees all seemed to be full of mirrors. And I mean all along River Road and up our slope. Definitely, that light was what gave me the headache. By the time I reached my own gate, I thought surely I was going to faint, so I quickly put out my hand for balance. That was when I felt something move in front of me, as if someone was stepping away. So, startled, I looked around at once. Don't know what I thought, but, eh, what was that? I asked myself. You see how I wasn't so superstitious as to jump to conclusions right away. I even wondered if maybe because of the headache, I was hallucinating-lah. Because of course, there seemed to be nothing there. Only the light and my headache, both getting worse.

There was no one in front of the gate—I remember staring at the gate design. You know our gate design. Every house still has the same one, with the four watchful dragons. My Hock Siew used to say that the architect or the contractor or whoever designed this neighborhood must have been very Chinese, that's why all the gates have dragons. But, you know, seems to me there could be another reason also. Remember how, according to Malay folklore, dragons guarded the Pauh Janggi during the days of Creation? Of course, that's Malay folklore, but so what? That's the tree-lah, supposed to be buried somewhere in the Indian Ocean, not far off the coast of Sumatra. Rumor has it, the Bataks used to gather the fruits when they broke loose and floated to the surface. To sell, of course. Supposedly, the fruits looked just like coconuts and had powerful medicinal properties. I don't see any contradiction with the Bible, so who can say the story's not true?

But my Hock Siew didn't like looking at the dragons. That's why he had our gate repainted black. See how in the daytime, only when you stare at it a while, then you can see the dragons? Otherwise, the gate looks like repeated pattern and that's all. Black also helps with the dust, you know.

So, as I was saying, I could see there was no one in front of the gate. Nor was there anyone on the road, no one anywhere. Not even Gopal Dharma, who was living next door, was outside watering his precious fruit trees. According to the time, which was around half-past nine, I think, he at least should have been in the garden, watering his beloved trees. But that morning, you know, he wasn't.

So then, I reached through the gate to unlatch it, and again something moved past my face, like a whitish, transparent figure or shadow crossing in front of me. Then I knew.

Quickly, I made the sign of the cross. I began to pray, Our Father, who art in heaven, hallowed be Thy name—as I opened the gate. I didn't stop praying until I was inside the house. Then I locked both the front and back doors, and I hurried upstairs. Don't ask why I thought locking the doors could keep out the ghost, but that's what I did.

He didn't follow me in.

Luckily I always kept my rosary on top of my bureau so that morning there it was, waiting for me. I grabbed it and went to lie down. For some reason, I began with the Sorrowful Mysteries. Normally I would have started with the Joyful Mysteries, because of course, that's the way Our Lord's life started, with the Angel Gabriel appearing to the Blessed Virgin while she was praying, and then St. John the Baptist leaping in his mother Elizabeth's womb when he felt his mother's sister coming up the road, and so on. But as I was saying, I was led to pray the Sorrowful Mysteries, instead. Of course, the Holy Spirit was using me as a vessel, but I didn't realize it at the time. I was quite frightened, you know. Already Auntie Coco's sister had vanished without a trace. Now with that ghost waiting for me outside the gate—for all I knew, it could be a spirit from the Abyss.

What if that same ghost had been waiting outside Auntie Coco's gate? The sister, with her lopsided brain, she wouldn't have known not to follow him. Those were my thoughts while I was praying. See-lah how weak my faith was, exactly one-mustard-seed size.

VALERIE NAIR

daughter of william and amy chan

mother of shakilah

H ER FIRST MORNING, the angsana tree was full of rain outside the window, the gray sky bursting with lightning. Eleven chickens drowned that morning, in the water lily pond. No one knew where they had come from, how they could have been smuggled into the hospital garden without anyone noticing. We didn't know if this was an ill omen or a lucky sign. Some of Ben's aunts thought it was lucky. It meant Shakilah would have an extraordinary life, they said. But I wasn't so sure. It was the first important fact of Shakilah's life, and it was out of our hands. Imagine knowing this as a mother. Imagine if you had given birth to your daughter on such a day, how closely you would have watched her, your eyes hiding in her shadow day after day, until your soul becomes like an onion, layered with the years of your daughter's life. She grows up, moves on, shedding her old skins, leaving them with you. Understand how it was. Think what it took for me to send her away. I didn't know if I would have the strength a second time.

Those details, as I was saying. Maybe it was wrong for me to go through her things, but truly I felt I had no choice. She wasn't telling me the truth, as if I wouldn't know, as if I couldn't hear the doors snapping shut in her mind as she spoke. The way she had hesitated before telling me the father's name was Marlowe, I knew what she was thinking—that if she gave me a ridiculous name like that, I would believe her. She had forgotten whom she was talking to. Now that she herself was carrying, she should have known. I was the one who had carried her. I knew before she said, "His name is Marlowe," it was a lie. I could hear how she was swallowing her feelings, the same way as when she was a child. All her feelings, her true feelings. Everyone was fooled, except me. The rest didn't know. *Wah, you so blessed,* Ben's relatives used to say. *Such a happy girl you have. She never gets angry-ah? So good-natured.*

Why lie about his name? That was what had worried me. That was how I knew something more was up. Giving the father's real name would not have hurt him. If he were Singaporean, it would have been a different matter, because then there would be his reputation to consider, and if he were married, worse. I had considered that he might be married. Maybe he already had children. But he was in America. Nothing that happened here was going to touch him. Why go through the trouble of hiding his name? Especially since this was one lie that was doomed to show up as a lie, sooner or later. This baby was going to be born, and there was going to be a birth certificate to fill out. How far was Shakilah willing to go? Was she going to lie to her child as well? My grandchild. Imagine the love already planted in me for this sweet chiku in my daughter's womb.

When had I known she would be a girl? I knew it without having to put my hand on Shakilah's womb, which is the easiest way to tell with babies. But this one was my own granddaughter. I could hear her. Shakilah didn't know this, or if she did, she never let on that she knew. You were quiet. I didn't even know you were there. But your sister's soul could speak, and before she realized your mother didn't want her to speak to me, we were already communicating. No, not with words. Not her. Only I used words, because after birth, the body always needs words, when the soul goes into hiding. But your sister and her soul were still one entity. She didn't need words, yet. I could hear her clearly every time, like windy music, like rain on a leaf. Then suddenly she stopped. I kept calling to her, but she would not answer, and I didn't know why, at first. *Tell me why you're angry with me*, I asked her. So then she told me, and poor thing, I could feel her nervousness. I didn't ask her how she knew, because some things between mother and daughter mustn't be interfered with, and I thought I could set an example for her. I knew from the very beginning, for her own sake, there were questions she must never ask.

Nothing teaches like example. Understand what this means about why I tell the story this way.

So I had to find another way to find out who your father was. No, not to satisfy my own curiosity. This wasn't curiosity. I was taking an enormous risk when I went into your mother's room that day. We were already estranged. It wouldn't be an exaggeration for me to say we had spoken no more than twenty sentences to each other, in the whole week since she had come home. I didn't know why, but I could feel your mother's anger swimming around me. I wouldn't have gone into her room if it weren't out of necessity. Love was what led me there, love for her, love for your sister. How could I protect a granddaughter whose strengths and weaknesses I didn't know? Sometimes it's possible to foretell the evils that await a birth.

Think of inherited strengths as scars from previous births, like antibodies in the blood, left from battles fought by the ancestors when they themselves were born. That was what I was looking for. I was looking for clues.

SHAKILAH COULD HAVE hidden everything better. That was what made me wonder if she had suspected I might go through her things. Maybe she was hoping I would. I thought this at the time. I thought it was her way of telling me what she couldn't bring herself to say. Either she couldn't say it to me face to face, or she was afraid to hear her thoughts turned into words, afraid to give them that physical reality, so to speak. Words would harden them, surround them with borders and sharp corners. Words would imprison them. Shakilah knew the price of speech. She knew language was a cage with no door. Start speaking, and the only direction possible is forward, deeper into the cage. Speaking is not writing. Understand the difference. Writing happens between the body and the soul. Speaking happens outside the body, always threatening the soul, just as food threatens the body even as it feeds it. For all her Americanness, my daughter knew there was no such thing as free speech. Truly, it was just an American dream.

The matchbox was the easiest to find, lying in the side pocket of her satchel. Her satchel was lovely, all leather and well stitched, with three compartments on the inside, and five loops to hold her pens. That was how I knew she was doing well over there, so it wasn't a money situation that had brought her back. And the matchbox was a perplexing clue, obviously a souvenir, but very odd. When I picked it up, it seemed to glow for a moment, but I thought maybe it was just a trick of the light. This was around half-past twelve in the afternoon. The air was still damp from the previous night's rain, even though the ground outside looked dry, so the light felt strange, so glossy and fluid, a diaphanous film pressing over us. But it was only because of the dampness, I told myself. There was nothing wrong with the sun. I could see it overhead when I peered out of the window and looked up. There it was, that morning draped in a white circular mist suspended in the sky. The left eye of our first ancestor, the eye closer to the heart, understand. I had never seen it look like this, but truly, I thought nothing of it. No, I wasn't ignoring what had happened the previous night. Let me tell the story my own way.

The matchbox had been painted red, on the sides and on the back. On the front was a picture, also painted on, of a bride and bridegroom, holding hands inside a wavy border made with gold thread glued onto the box. It looked like a wedding picture to me because of the way they were dressed, the man in a black tuxedo, the woman in a red satin gown, and she wore flowers in her hair. Bougainvillea, I thought at once, even though the flowers were tiny. They had the fragile air of bougainvillea. The wall behind the woman's head was bright yellow, and decorated with a few floating leaves, dropping from a tree branch that wasn't in the picture. Both the man and the woman had black hair, and beige skin. I assumed they were American, maybe from California, where the climate's warm enough and sunny enough to grow bougainvillea.

So the father isn't blond. That was the first conclusion I drew, before looking inside the box. The second was that his eyes were not blue, because the man and the woman both had dark eyes. Then I pulled out the little drawer, because I could feel the weight of something rolling about inside.

There was a tiny transparent capsule containing reddish-brown dirt, a tiny doll made of threads of different colors, and a tiny strip of white paper, folded in half. Was the doll American voodoo? Knowing your mother, I wouldn't have been surprised, but when I moved my hand over the open drawer, I felt nothing. No energy from anyone's soul was trapped inside. Then I unfolded the strip of paper. On it was printed, *Leave the past behind.*

I looked at that sentence a long time. Then I folded the strip of paper and put it back into the box. I closed the drawer and dropped the box into the side pocket of the satchel, and I slid the satchel into the narrow space between the bureau and the bed, exactly where I had found it, I thought. Then I walked around the bed to where her suitcase was lying on top of her old desk. Shakilah still hadn't unpacked her clothes and most of her things were in the suitcase, so I opened it slowly. I felt underneath her clothes, slipping my fingers carefully between the layers so as not to ruffle them, and I found the other things, the other details of her life in America which she couldn't tell me about.

That was when I was forced to put two and two together.

NO, HER FRIEND Rose didn't know, even though she and your mother used to be best friends. Rose never had that kind of wildness in her, and with a mother like Helena, besides.

No wonder Eve would look so broken-hearted whenever I saw her. Back when Shakilah had first left, and the loneliness had been unbearable, the house so silent in the evenings, I used to go for walks. Sometimes if it was the right time, Eve would be outside her house, watering the jacaranda as usual. No wonder sometimes she would look up when I passed by, and look at me in that way. I had thought she understood my sorrow, and for a while, I was even afraid she might have guessed at the truth, because of the way she would look at me.

And all that while, she had been searching my face to see if I had guessed her secrets.

IMAGINE HAVING SOMETHING like that stab you in the back. Your daughter, your own daughter whom you've raised, whom you've gone through fire to protect, so to speak. You start wondering if you did it too late, if your lack of courage made you wait too long. And what about now? What should you do now? What should you do about your granddaughter?

So I knew why she was out for so long that morning, when she had gone for a walk by herself.

I could hear her and Rose talking downstairs when I woke up from my nap. (Zaida's daughter Mahani had also come over that day, but she had left by then.) I wasn't feeling refreshed, not at all. There was still a bit of a headache throbbing behind my eyelids, but it was faint, not the blinding pain that had built up while I was sitting in Shakilah's room earlier. I had never had a headache like that, arrows of pain shooting down my sides, into my arms and my thighs. And how my right hand had burned. A single sharp pain in it, like a red-hot iron needle passing through my palm. No, I had no explanation and I wasn't looking for one. *There are more things in heaven and earth, Mercutio, than are dreamt of in your philosophy.* No, Mercutio never heard those words, because he was in the other play with Romeo. But he, too, was fated to die. You see how we forget the one that's not directly in front of us. Yes, this story's wandering about a bit. Believe me, it's the only way.

At least, I had managed to sleep a bit. Always be thankful for small blessings.

THE WORST WAS yet to come. What was I being tested for? Or was it punishment? When she told me what she was thinking about, I was stunned. I couldn't speak for a few seconds. I could only stare at her, at this daughter who had grown within my womb, whose delicate head had once fit perfectly against my palm. When I used to cuddle her, my fingers would close so easily around the side of her head, and I would hold her like that, her earlobe rubbing on my middle fingertip, her skull so fragile beneath my thumb, I would check for marks whenever I put her down, nervous about leaving a bruise on her. This daughter I

FIONA CHEONG   87

used to sing to, very softly after Ben had fallen asleep, partly so as not to wake him, but also because I knew her eardrum was so tiny and new, I was afraid to burst it. This daughter, whom I had loved even before she was born. How could she say she didn't trust me? In a voice so empty, so devoid of feeling. Had she wandered so far from herself? What had happened to her soul in America? What was going to happen when she went back? Because no matter the cost, there was no question that she had to go back, I thought. Your mother was never safe here. Even she knew it. The question was how not to give in to my longing to keep her home, especially now that she seemed so lost, and with another life to think about. Another soul, not yet born and still tender. And I didn't even know about you.

What did Shakilah mean, she didn't trust me? That was what I was wondering when she said it.

"You know what I mean, Mama."

She must have read the question in my eyes. Shock and confusion had paralyzed my face. She could see that, obviously. She must have expected it. She had even hoped for it, I thought, as I looked at her sitting there on the couch, with her hands folded in her lap, as if she were demure and ladylike, which as a teenager she had never been. I could see she was a woman now, your mother. I could feel within her the wall surrounding her soul, so that I could no longer reach it. Within that wall was a desert so bleak like the Gobi, miles of dusty sand where her soul was wandering. Was she going to take her daughter's soul there as well? *Mama, if something happens to me, I want Eve Thumboo to take care of my baby. I've already asked her.* Not a shiver in Shakilah's voice when she had said that, when she had looked me straight in the eye and informed me she was going to give away my granddaughter, and not only that, but give her away to the woman who had already grabbed one child from me.

Finally, I found my voice, but it was shaky. "I don't know what you mean," I told her. "Tell me what you mean, Shakilah."

She just looked at me.

It was close to six o'clock. Rose had left around half-past five, with a sheepish expression on her face as she apologized for not being able to stay for dinner that evening. Now I knew why. Helena herself had stopped by with Bernadette, under the pretense of bringing over some of her pineapple tarts for Shakilah. Wait till they found out about this, I thought. My headache was building up again, a dull pain this time, a sluggish ache centered in my crown and sending thin roots down. I could feel the darkness that was coming as I shut my eyes for a moment. The night was already moving through the trees, heaving against our walls. The pain ripped through my shoulders. I felt it enter my chest, but it didn't go lower than my navel.

"Shall I get you some aspirin?" Shakilah asked, but her voice didn't sound willing or concerned. It sounded exhausted, fed up, even though she was trying to hide it. As a mother, you can hear.

I shook my head and opened my eyes. Outside, the air still carried a dim light, the paltry glow of the sun as it was going down, but in the living room twilight had already arrived. I thought about switching on the lamp on the end table beside me, but my arms felt heavy. I thought, what would be the point? I was also afraid of what else I might see in your mother's eyes, if the light in the room grew brighter. I couldn't look at her anymore. I stared at my hands. How ugly they had become, how dry and old and useless. As always, I was aware of not wearing my wedding ring. At least, I didn't have to wear it anymore. Shakilah must have noticed this, but she hadn't said a word about it.

I heard her sigh. "Are you sure you don't want some aspirin?" she asked, and I made myself speak.

"No, I don't want any aspirin," I said. I could hear the quake in my voice, even though I had tried to speak steadily.

She sighed again. What was she sighing for? I was the one being pierced. To have to live out the rest of your days hearing your granddaughter call the wrong woman Grandma. Imagine it. That Jezebel, holding my granddaughter's hand, teaching her things.

Not to mention the immense shame. How would I show my face around the neighborhood, hold my head up amidst the buzzing gossip, the pity, everyone glancing sideways and not daring to speak to me? Had she thought about that? Had she thought what a sword she was driving through my soul? Wasn't it enough that I was already enduring her shame? Shakilah wasn't deaf. She could hear the whispers that had been travelling up and down the road all week, some of them directed at me. *Eh, the apple doesn't fall far from the tree.* She must have known before she came home what would happen. Arriving with her belly so ripe, her left hand empty.

"What did I do?" I asked her, trying again to hold my voice steady. "What has made you so angry with me, Shakilah?"

"You know," she said, quite sharply. Then she looked at me, as if she had been waiting a long time for me to ask her that question. Now she was waiting for me to say something else, but I didn't know what she was referring to at all.

"No." I shook my head. "No, darling, I don't know."

"You know," she said again, defiantly and suddenly sounding just like Ben, in the old days when Ben and I were dating, when we were young and innocent, and he was still sweet, and in love with me. Those were the old days. Life changes. Or maybe it was marriage that had changed us, Ben and me, or just age. I never knew what had made him start looking at me differently, and in the end, it didn't matter. What I did, I had to do. But Shakilah didn't know about any of it. I was sure she didn't know what I had done to save her. I had been very careful. I hadn't wanted her to carry the burden of knowing.

"What is it?" I asked, and I tried to sound gentle and loving. "Please tell me, darling." I wanted her to understand I was her mother, that I would do anything for her, even though the truth was that I wasn't feeling very strong, and my hands were trembling.

"You think I don't remember." Her voice was almost a whisper. I saw her take in a deep breath, and then she went on, "I remember."

I didn't know what she was talking about.

"I thought it was a dream. I thought I dreamt it."

Now I thought I knew the incident to which she was referring, but I still didn't know why she was angry at me, unless she was blaming me for allowing it to happen. Was that it? I didn't want to interrupt her, so I tried to study her face. But Shakilah was looking down at her hands, and even in the dimness in the room, the last vestiges of daylight ebbing away fast, I could sense the deadening between us. It was as if blood and air had left your mother's body, as if her bones and skin were only remnants of the child I had carried. Only her soul was still wandering, blowing about like a piece of seashell in that desert that was inside her. I didn't know what to do, except sit there and wait for whatever else was coming, and accept it. At my age, I could feel fate's hand when it reached in. Maybe guilt had something to do with it. Maybe. Yes, you always have guilt, even when you know you had no choice.

"Children don't have such dreams. Or if they do, they're signs. The dreams are signs."

She sounded as if she had turned into a stranger, right before my eyes. That was how she sounded. On the surface, nothing was changing. She looked the same, with Ben's thick eyelashes and his thick hair, which his relatives had been so happy about, even if she wasn't his coloring. Not that they had ever mentioned it—the only time his relatives had shown some discretion. But I had seen it on their faces, right from the start. As soon as they had left the hospital room, they must have told one another, *Aiya, lucky. The girl has her father's looks.* Yes, my feelings were hurt, but I was able to convince myself it was okay. As long as Ben loved me, who cared if his relatives didn't find me pretty enough for him? But it was a relief to cut them off after the funeral, not to have to keep tolerating their insults and accusations. They hadn't wanted me to send Shakilah away, especially to America, by herself. If Ben hadn't been so ill, they would have succeeded in stopping me. Yes, they would have, because it would have been them against me. My relatives? No need to ask about them. They've never been involved.

I wondered if your sister was awake, listening to what was going on between her mother and her grandmother. She was going to be a beautiful child. I already knew it, her soul untainted like the first soul in Paradise, her goodness intact like a butterfly's body curled up in its cocoon, like a flower before it buds. But she was staying so quiet, now I couldn't tell if she was awake.

"You put your hand between my legs."

Imagine a mother hearing those words from her own daughter. Even if you've been waiting for them, you're not prepared. She had never talked about it. The doctors at Mount Alvernia had told me the wound was small, it would heal. *She's lucky. Whoever did this could have killed her, if he went deeper.* We didn't know if she would even remember. I had hoped she wouldn't. Halimah had said she might not, and I had hoped for it. But I must have known that it was impossible, that her body was marked, her mind ravaged beyond repair. I wasn't surprised to hear her speak about it, finally. What I wasn't expecting was where it would lead.

"You thought I was asleep. I wasn't."

She was still looking at her hands, trying to find in herself what was no longer there, I thought. A stolen beginning. A stolen home. My poor darling.

"I wasn't asleep. I know what you did, Mama."

At first, I couldn't respond. I thought I must have misheard her. But I had been listening too carefully to have done that. "What are you saying?" I asked her. "Do you hear what you're saying?"

"You put your hand between my legs."

"No."

"How could you do such a thing?"

Was she mad? Had she gone mad? "No," I repeated. "I didn't do that to you. Listen to me, Shakilah. I didn't do that to you." I kept shaking my head, as if that would make her believe me. She wasn't even looking at me.

"You put your hand between my legs," she said a third time, still looking down at her hands, not at me. "How old was I? Four? Five? You thought I wouldn't remember."

She was confused, I thought. Perhaps she had woken up once while I was putting on the ointment, even though I would wait until she was fast asleep each time. Had she been asleep when he touched her? I had never found out for sure, understand. Halimah hadn't said it was Ben, and if it was, surely I had acted in time.

No, Halimah had seen to it that the powder she gave me would not stop his heart, but his hands could do nothing. Not anymore.

"You. It was you."

"Darling, no."

"Mama, it was you."

Was it why then, she was the way she was, her passions straying off in their unnatural direction? But if she believed it was I who had committed such an abhorrent act, how could she bear to have more women touch her? How could she bear to touch them herself? In her anger?

Eve's hand. Eve's fingers caressing her skin. The thought of it sickened me. With my granddaughter helpless in the womb, able to hear everything. I had to shut my eyes, and breathe deeply so as not to faint.

"Why did you do it?" Her voice was hardly a sigh. My Shakilah. My darling girl. Was the other one also my age? Were all of them? How many had there been? There must have been more than one. It was America.

I couldn't stand it anymore. To have it come to this, after all the fear and suffering and loneliness and waiting, just waiting, for someone to find out. To have her lying down with women out of some kind of revenge directed at me, because she thought I was the one. Not even women her age, but women too old for men, ugly hags, and all the hungrier for it. Their fingers. Imagine their fingers, hard, skeletal, clawing at her. Imagine their mouths, their dry breath. Greedy. I had done this to my daughter. Somehow, it was my doing.

I got up. I went straight upstairs to the bathroom, my head and chest pounding, my stomach nauseous. I closed the door because I didn't want her to hear me. I didn't want her sympathy.

All I wanted now was my granddaughter. A chance to live out my years as a grandmother with a child who loved me. It was a simple wish. It was all I wanted. Was it so much to ask for?

HELENA SIM

YOU KNOW THE story of Pontianak, right? She was stillborn, the daughter of the first Langsuir. Aiya, you don't know what a Langsuir is? Ya-lah, a vampire. Legend has it she was living as an ordinary lady at the time, Pontianak's mother, but with extraordinary beauty-lah, and maybe that was the reason for her misfortune. Because when she found out that her baby was stillborn, and then, worse, had become Pontianak, a vampire doomed to prey on women in labor, the shock of it was so great, she died. To this day, no one knows who performed black magic on her baby. But if you want my opinion, I can tell you some other lady must have been too jealous of the Langsuir's beauty. Maybe Pontianak's father was hanky-pankying around, who knows? Ah, so anyway, young people nowadays, they call it superstition, but it's true, you know. Pontianak exists. This is not just some old wives' tale, okay? Any time a woman gives birth, the family better be careful. Especially if they know beforehand the birth is going to be difficult, that could be a sign-lah. Pontianak and her mother are always waiting, you know. Together, the two of them. Ya-lah, that was why the mother became a Langsuir again, so she could be with her daughter. According to legend, what she did was clap her hands. Imagine-lah, if you had been in the room with her, watching her clap her hands when her baby was dead. Her relatives must have known at once something odd was happening. That was how she became the first Langsuir-lah. After clapping her hands, suddenly she screeched like an owl and flew out the window into a tree.

"That's folklore only," Bernadette said to me, when I tried to explain. That coconut-head. Folklore doesn't mean it's not true, but she was always like that, ever since I've known her. Forever trying to be skeptical, just for the sake of being skeptical.

"Alamak, these are warning signs, Bernadette," I said, trying to keep my patience. What I meant was this. Something fishy was going on in the spirit world, and what with Valerie's daughter coming home pregnant like that. Life isn't that full of coincidences, okay? But who knew whether Valerie herself was putting two and two together. Probably not, so someone better warn her, bukan? No? Mothers are full of blind spots. But that Bernadette, she refused to see my logic.

"We don't know what's going on between those two," she said. "Fifteen years that girl refused to come home. Who knows why. Now you want to go and interfere. You gila?"

"Warning is not interfering, okay?" I said.

"Aiya, I tell you that story's just a legend-lah," she said. "I never believed it, okay?"

"Eh, you liar," I said. That Bernadette, she couldn't fool me, after all our years of knowing each other. I asked her, "So now you want me to think the ghost this morning was just my imagination?"

She didn't want to answer, but I knew what she was thinking. That was just my luck-lah. To be honest, Bernadette wouldn't have been my first choice to tell about my experience. But what to do, she was the only one who happened to be around that afternoon. I was desperate, okay? I didn't wake up from my nap until half-past two. See what a deep sleep I had fallen into, just as if I had been put under a spell. Rose had already come home and gone out again, all without my knowing. The last thing I wanted was to be left by myself the rest of the day. So, that was why I started calling people, and just my luck, Dorothy and Siew Chin both were out clothes shopping. I was a bit upset with them, you know, Dorothy and Siew Chin. Why hadn't they called to ask if I wanted to go? But the two of them could be like that sometimes. Sometimes they would go out just so Siew Chin could complain to Dorothy ad infinitum about Jeremy. Since Hock Siew and I had had the perfect marriage, they didn't want me along-lah. Of course I knew this. Ah, so anyway, no one answered the phone except Bernadette. (I don't think Dorothy's girl was home, that Lulu Mendez. Unless maybe she was off in her room with her nose in a book.) So this was how come I was stuck with Bernadette-lah.

"Can't be-lah," she said suddenly.

"Can't be what?" I asked. "What can't be?"

"That poor girl kena kidnapped-lah. Poor thing. What I don't understand is, how come Auntie Coco just left her alone outside the house?"

From the look on Bernadette's face I knew what she was referring to, and also because one way or another, she was always bringing up the topic. So I said, "You and your slave ships."

And see, was I right on target or not? Immediately Bernadette said, "That's not just a rumor, okay? You don't remember the newspapers, is it?"

See-lah how she was. That rumor was over long ago, okay? Back in 1976, or was it 1977? Somewhere around that time, when young girls kept disappearing and nobody could find them, people were saying they had been kidnapped and taken to Thailand, to be sold as sex slaves-lah. How that story ever made it into the newspapers, I don't know. As far as I knew then and as far as I know now, it was just gossip, what. Ya, ya, there are different levels of gossip, it's true, depending on how much proof you have. And say, okay-lah, giving Bernadette her due, say, I admit it was possible. Indonesia's comprised of so many islands, anything could happen there, in the outer islands especially. Ya, I'm sure there are girls who have disappeared whom we don't know about, but as for the exact nature of their misfortune? Let's put it this way, there was more than one possibility, okay? All those aboriginal tribes still living in the jungle? Even today, you can find headhunters there. And with young people, every generation's the same. Most of them are so careless. Carefree and careless. Now they even go hiking in the jungle, in all that heat and with the mosquitoes and all those fires burning. Maybe those who disappeared in the past were also trying to go hiking, or were lured out there by their boyfriends. Who's to know? So imagine one young girl if she bodoh-bodoh wasn't watching where she stepped and crossed into their territory, ah, habis. Finished-lah. Even if she wasn't alone, it can happen so fast, you know. One second she's there, next second she's gone. In the blink of an eye, as they say. (That's why I used to tell Rose, if she wanted to travel, go ahead. Save up her money and see the world, but stay out of Indonesia. Nothing to see there, anyway. But she didn't have the travelling bug, always wanting to stay home only.)

"You don't listen to legends, you listen to rumors?" I said to Bernadette.

"Please-lah, Helena, I'm fifty-eight years old. How I'm going to believe in Pontianak?"

Alamak, when she said that, I wanted to roll my eyes just like Rose sometimes used to roll her eyes at me. Honestly, I almost did it, you know. "So, you're fifty-eight years old," I said. As if I was just a spring chicken-lah. "So what?"

"So this is what." And that Bernadette, she leaned forward towards me as if she was about to drop all kinds of pearls of wisdom on my dining table. That was the look that was on her face now. "I myself have never seen Pontianak," she said. "And I myself don't know anyone who has seen her. You?"

I just sighed, at that point.

"Well, Helena?" So profound she thought she was being, you see? But now that my patience was being tested to its limits, desperate or not, I had to give her some of her own medicine.

"Have you ever seen the Holy Spirit?" I said. Ah, I thought that would shut her up, but no, she was going strong, that Bernadette.

"That's not the same thing," she said. "You are a Catholic, not a Muslim."

"So what do you mean?" I said.

"When you're a Catholic, that means you know in your heart the Holy Spirit exists. Did Jesus ever say anything about Pontianak?"

"He talked about demons, okay?"

"Ya, so? Those were Satan's cohorts, of course."

"Oh, and I suppose Pontianak couldn't have been one of them. You've asked Jesus this yourself, right?"

See that Bernadette. Always she would rattle my nerves eventually. Enough was enough, I was thinking. But then, luckily, I remembered she had been home the previous night, which Bernadette had told me as soon as I called, so I stopped my tongue from going on. As much as I didn't want to admit it, she had a bit of knowledge that I needed, okay? I couldn't rely on Winifred Teo's story only. So now I was forced to act like a hypocrite. Quickly better offer her some pineapple tarts, I thought to myself. Luckily, I had been baking just the previous afternoon, so my tarts were still quite fresh. Plus, anyone would tell you, Helena Sim's pineapple tarts are A-number one. That's the truth. I'm not boasting, okay? (Ask Rose, who never praises me if she can help it, I don't know why she has to be so modest, but you know you can believe her.)

Don't get the wrong idea. Bernadette and I never went overboard, okay, with our disagreements. People our age can't afford to lose the friends they have. Any of our hearts could stop at any time.

So, she was still there when it happened. This must have been around four o'clock or a bit after. I was getting up from the table to go into the kitchen because I was going to boil more water for tea, and Bernadette was reaching for her third pineapple tart. You know that bottomless stomach of hers, especially when it comes to my delicious tarts. She was eating like a teenager that afternoon. So, the whole time we were in the dining room, which meant, of course, we could see the road. See how in most of our houses, the dining room is off to the side of the living room? Ask Bernadette to confirm this-lah, if you want. Ask her to tell you how without rhyme or reason, the weather outside changed. This time I wasn't the only eye-witness, okay?

IT HAPPENED ONLY for a minute-lah. That's why it's so hard to confirm. It's easy to say those of us who saw were hallucinating, easy to blame the heat also. But here's the truth. All that brightness outside, suddenly the sun was gone. In a flash, as they say. One minute it was the middle of the afternoon, hot as usual, next minute, the air became so dark, it could have been midnight, okay? Like an eclipse-lah. Suddenly I thought, now I know what an eclipse means. The whole world around us vanishing. Ah, like that. The road, the graveyard, Gopal Dharma's fruit trees next door, all gone. Bernadette, I remember, she called out right away, "Eh, Alamak, apa 'tu?" Every time that Bernadette panics, she forgets her English, ya? Ah, so anyway, if not for her voice, I also would have panicked. Instead, I said, "Didn't I tell you? This is what you get for not believing me." And of course, that Bernadette, now what could she say? Serves her right for being so stubborn in her thinking. Coconut-head. Those were my thoughts. See how calm I was. The Holy Spirit must have been with me, because of the rosary I was praying earlier. See how important it is to have even a bit of faith.

So, the darkness lasted for a minute, and then everything went back to normal.

Bernadette, she was completely in shock. Like a statue she was, sitting in her chair. She couldn't move, just stared at me, and her face so puchat. As if she had seen the Devil, that's how pale she was, white as flour. I almost pitied her, you know. Myself, maybe the morning's experience had prepared me a bit. That must have been it. I could feel my heart beating quite fast, but I wasn't tongue-tied, as Rose would say. I wasn't paralyzed. I just put one foot in front of the other and when I was in the kitchen, I picked up the kettle, filled it with water, and put it on the stove, just as if everything was normal. I remember looking at the clock as I was turning on the burner. It was exactly ten minutes past four. Then while the water was heating up, I went back out to the dining area.

Bernadette was breathing again, slowly but surely, but she still couldn't talk, and I knew from the way she looked at me, she was wondering how come I was being so calm. Of course, that's how she was interpreting my behavior. Anyone else who had known me that long would have known that was my way of gathering my thoughts. But you know her. She was never that observant of other people-lah.

"Didn't I tell you?" I said to her. I couldn't resist it. "You still want to say it's all coincidence?"

Imagine how shocked she was, that Bernadette, she couldn't respond to my teasing even. Of course I was trying to provoke her, to bring her back to normal. But all she could do was stare at me, sit and stare, sit and stare. That's all. Completely useless.

So I left her alone, for a while. When the water boiled, I went to make tea, and then I came back to the table with two cups and we just sat there, Bernadette and I, drinking our tea silently until she was ready to talk. Now and then I would look outside, just in case something else was going to happen, although my instincts told me that was it for the day. And of course I was right. Nothing else happened, except once I saw Adelaide's grandson, Nathan, walking past. That must have been around half-past four, and he was carrying a cake. Looked like a butter cake or a pound cake, and ah, just like that, the whole cake on a plate in the open air. You see how those Eurasians are. Dust everywhere, they don't care. I'm sure Adelaide could have found a Tupperware container or something, or borrowed one. But her intentions were good-lah. The cake must have been for Auntie Coco. (Must sound a bit funny, all of us calling Auntie Coco that way—she must have been my age, maybe younger even, but a habit's a habit-lah.) So anyway, nothing else happened. The weather stayed warm and sunny, back to humid, and then there was a small breeze. I could hear it in Gopal Dharma's fruit trees. It made the air a bit soothing, his leaves rustling in the breeze.

Otherwise, I was looking at Bernadette. To be honest, I was a bit worried for her. She was never as tough as the rest of us, you know. She must have inherited her mother's health-lah. You know her mother died quite young, I think at forty-plus years old. Weak heart, we all heard. Bernadette, she was always the same way. Even in our younger days, she never ran about or played rough games. Even though obviously she had outlived her mother's age, these things, who can say. So I watched her carefully. She better not keel over in my house, I thought. After everything, I didn't need that kind of luck, to have someone die in my house, even a friend. This isn't superstition, okay? Ya, ya, it must sound like a contradiction. If I knew Bernadette's health history, why I always argued with her? But that's how old friends are, ya? Also, given Bernadette's personality, how to treat her like gold? She didn't inspire that kind of treatment, you know. (Nowadays, I've learned patience, but see how long it takes to learn patience.)

"Okay-lah," she said, finally, her voice tired.

"Okay?" I said. "Okay what?" See how mean I could be, I don't know why.

"Tell me one more time-lah," she said.

Still, I didn't say anything, even though of course I knew what she meant. I'm not slow, okay?

"What happened this morning, Helena," she said. "Tell me again-lah. I don't think I was listening very well before."

Ah, now she had given in completely, now I was satisfied. So childish of me, ya? But that's how I was-lah, in those days. That's how I used to be.

ANYWAY. MY FEELING about the slave ships was that if, really, Indonesians were selling our girls to the Thais, the government would have found out already. You know how money-minded our government is. There's no way any kind of trading could have gone on without their knowing about it eventually, okay? (The same goes-lah for the pirate ships, if you ever hear that rumor being revived, about how in the outer islands, there may still be tribes of pirates. That for sure I don't know, but somehow I doubt it. Headhunters and Pontianak herself, those are different matters entirely.)

So I went through my story another time for Bernadette, and she just listened, and at the end of it, I asked her did she want to go with me to warn Valerie Nair. She said okay. Ah, just like that.

Okay. To be honest, I didn't expect her to agree so fast. But never look a gift horse in the mouth, ya? So off we went-lah, and on the way, I asked her to tell me her version of what had happened the previous night. And here's the strange part. Everything was the same as in Winifred Teo's story, except Bernadette couldn't remember whether or not Adelaide's grandson was with her when she came outside. And yet Winifred had said specifically that Nathan had been one of the witnesses, because she was surprised at how tall he had grown. Standing next to Adelaide, he was almost one whole head taller already, Winifred had said to me, as if I hadn't noticed for myself how tall the boy was. You see how children grow.

But anyway, Bernadette couldn't remember seeing him. "I don't think he was there, Helena," she said to me, as we were walking on the road. "Funny, why I don't remember?"

Between Bernadette and Winifred, how was I going to choose whom to believe? So I decided to wait for Rose. It didn't seem important-lah, at the time, and I was already starting to lean more towards Winifred, because as I've pointed out, Bernadette couldn't always be trusted to notice things, okay?

GILA! HAVE YOU lost your mind? How can you let her go by her-self? What kind of mother are you? Those had been the accu-sations, Ben's relatives descending like vultures. Ever since Shakilah was born, they had had their eyes on her, the first niece, the first granddaughter. Ben had accused me of overre-acting. He never saw them for what they were, vultures. But then, that was his family. He had been an only son, everyone's favorite nephew, the eldest grandchild, handsome and deeply beloved. No wife could have lived up to the expectations every-one must have had, what's more a Eurasian Chinese. I used to think about asking them if they realized that's what Shakilah was, a Eurasian Chinese, but for Ben's sake, and then for Shakilah's, I had held my tongue. *Do you know what can happen to her over there? A single girl like that?* They never understood. So locked within their own preconceptions, they never saw how Shakilah's protection had always been foremost on my mind. Such chagrin and outrage at her name, when I had chosen it. *That's a Muslim name! Why are you giving her a Muslim name?* How relieved I had been that Ben had believed me when I said I was naming Shakilah after my closest childhood friend, whose family had moved away when we were ten. He was too pragmatic in his nature to have understood why some babies must be disguised. But some of his aunts could have guessed at this, if their minds had been open to the possibility that they might not know everything.

Sooner or later, they were going to find out she was back. The word was going to spread, even though none of them lived nearby. Everyone talks on an island this small. Here, you can get family news from strangers.

How was I going to protect a granddaughter if I couldn't even say she was mine? And what had Shakilah told Eve about me? Was I going to be forbidden to be near the baby?

Fate's hand, as I was saying. You have to know when to preserve your energy. I leaned over the sink and washed my face. Before going back downstairs, I went into my room to put on some powder.

A sparrow was perched on the windowsill near my bureau when I entered the room, and my mind drifted towards Halimah. But it was only habit that made me think the sparrow might be something other than a sparrow. Yes, I'm sure. She would have been too busy at the time to bother with us, especially since she had warned me from the start not to marry Ben.

I combed my hair, and I changed my blouse. Never look as though you've surrendered, understand.

"DON'T WORRY, I'M not going to tell the world," Shakilah said, while she was washing the rice. She didn't look up.

I listened to the grains falling between her fingers, their sound like a rain shower in the rice pot. She swirled them around a few more times in the water, then drained the water out, holding her palm against the rim of the pot. Strange as this may sound, it gave me comfort to see her washing rice. You've heard what they say about Americans, how they don't wash their rice because they think they'll wash away the vitamins. Imagine that. Cooking rice without washing it first. Not that I had wanted Shakilah to stay exactly the same. I had known when she left that she would change. And no, I don't regret it, and I didn't even then. I would have paid any price for her safety.

"I'm not worried about that," I said, even though I was.

"That's because you know I would never tell," she said, her voice carrying no feeling at all. It drifted about the room like a splinter, or an old scab, a flake of skin that had fallen off her body, with nothing attached. And only the air was holding it up, as if the air were water, as if again, we were separated by water.

So you see, life hands you what it will. Better to accept it and make your peace, than to try to alter your fate. I had known this when I married Ben, and yet, I had married him. He and I weren't meant to be. His being too handsome for me had been a sign. Halimah had tried her best to persuade me. *Keep the baby. You want the baby, keep her. Leave the father alone.* But to become an unwed mother? Especially in those days? I wasn't brave enough. I was only sixteen.

"Are you going to keep avoiding the police?" she asked, as I opened the refrigerator and reached for some watercress. That had always been her favorite vegetable, the only vegetable I could get her to eat without her trying to spit it out, when she was a child.

She must have thought my fear was that somehow or other, the police would find out what I had done, what she believed I had done. Would it be easier on her if she knew the actual crime? What about your sister? What if she were to hear the truth about her mother, and about her grandmother, and about her grandfather? It was going to be bad enough when she found out about her father. Your mother didn't have to tell me the father's sperm had come from a sperm bank. I knew, now.

"I don't have anything to tell them about Auntie Coco and her sister," I said, pretending that was what your mother had meant with her question. "I can't tell them anything that would help them."

Not that I wasn't concerned about Auntie Coco, but I knew eventually she would realize her sister was all right. She would feel it.

Shakilah didn't ask anything else or say anymore after that. We did the rest of our cooking in silence, with the night outside like a black cloth moving over the grass. Once, I thought I heard a dog barking, and as we were setting the table, one of the neighbors' children shouted something up the road. That was when I checked Shakilah's face to see what her reaction was, but your mother's face was a closed book to me now, and I couldn't tell if she had even heard the shout.

Other than that, the night passed peacefully for us. (No, it didn't rain again, and Elizabeth Sandhu didn't stop by as she had on the previous night. Yes, she used to be Shakilah's favorite teacher at St. Agnes, but I'm quite sure there was no dirty business going on between them. Not Elizabeth. Don't go off on that wild goose chase. She had stopped by only for a brief visit, around nine o'clock. Yes, the police had left by then. No, no, there was nothing odd about Elizabeth's being in the neighborhood. She was simply visiting her in-laws on River Road.)

WHAT ELSE HAD I found in Shakilah's suitcase? A booklet with an American Indian man on the cover. He was carrying a spear and dancing on the grass, and the words *Santa Fe Visitors Guide* were strung out above his head. Two postcards, one showing a field of yellow wildflowers with purple mountains in the distance. The other showed an underground room, with a wooden ladder leading up to an open door in the ceiling, which seemed to be made of tree branches. Light from outside was falling into the room, throwing the shape of the door onto the wall behind the ladder.

And there was a third postcard, obviously local. On the front was an artist's rendition of the *Malay Great Argus*, which was the title printed underneath the picture. There were two beautifully painted argus pheasants, male and female, with the male in his glory. He was parading about and showing off his feathers while the female eyed him across the jungle clearing. The background showed a gauzy screen of pastel greens and blues, with the shapes of fallen tree trunks fading into the shadows. I took down for your sister the historical information given on the back of the postcard, so here it is: *The male great argus pheasant exhibits one of the most spectacular courtship displays of the bird world. Their enormous secondaries and intricately patterned primary wing feathers are masterpieces of nature's elaborate design. The two central tail feathers will grow to a length of 4 feet in the male. Due to the large amount of tree cutting in Malaysia, the wild habitat so necessary for this species to survive is now being seriously threatened.* Nothing about the female, naturally.

Yes, there was handwriting on the postcard. Of course it wasn't the same as the handwriting on the backs of the American postcards.

I found a handkerchief, too. It was ironed and folded into a small square, and hidden between the pages of the booklet. A yellow handkerchief, with scalloped edges trimmed in blue thread, and an embroidered fuchsia flower in each corner. Underneath one flower was the alphabet C, sewn in yellow thread as if to camouflage it.

No, don't ask me what the handwriting said. And no, there were no photographs. Not one.

HELENA SIM

N O-LAH, NO ONE was surprised when Benjamin Nair passed away. We never knew what exactly was wrong with him, but for how long already he had been sickly, at least eight or nine years, okay? Always in and out of Mount Alvernia. First, because of terrible headaches, so everyone suspected a brain tumor. But nothing showed up on the CAT scan, bukan? And then, when the fellow started tripping over nothing and falling down for no reason, still, the doctors couldn't come up with anything definite. Ya-lah, a bit of rumor was already going around that something else must be involved. Since Mount Alvernia's a Catholic hospital, if you can't get well there, gone case-lah. Ah, I remember that's what Dorothy and Siew Chin they all were saying when it happened, Bernadette even. But you see how I never jump to conclusions unnecessarily. I was the only one who disagreed, okay? Even though there was a logic to what they were saying, about black magic being involved. You can't find a holier hospital than Mount Alvernia. Nuns on every floor. (I've already told Rose, when my time comes, that's where I want to go. Lucifer better not get my soul in the final hour. Hopefully she was listening. You never know what that one might try when you're feeling weak. Look how he tried to go for Our Lord himself when Our Lord was feeling faint from hunger. Not shy, that Lucifer. Going for the Son of God, imagine). So anyway, none of us were surprised when the fellow finally went. But what I told the others at the time was that he must have had very poor nutrition as a child, and eventually that sort of thing catches up with you, you know.

Siew Chin may have been the one to mention the other possibility, or it could have been Bernadette. That part of my memory is a bit blurry, but that's the only part. (Don't ask Rose about this. Of course she'll tell you something different. From her point of view, even believing in miracles is superstitious. She didn't use to be like that, okay? I don't know what's happening with her nowadays.)

Anyway, Benjamin Nair's death was in 1980, during the third-year anniversary of my own Hock Siew's passing. Ah, so the experience of losing a husband was still fresh for me, bukan? I knew how Valerie was feeling. That was why I tried to get her involved in activities right away. But she didn't want-lah. Some women, you know how they are. Once the heart gets broken, it stays broken. Not that I'm saying this was what happened with Valerie. Who can say what happened? She didn't confide in us. (Just like that Madeleine Bhanu, when her Richard finally ran off with his secretary. Everyone knew it would happen, okay? Women with husbands like that should be more prepared, but they never are.) So anyway, she was quite a loner, Valerie. So the rumors were bound to gather, right? That's why I never shut myself away. If you don't want people to talk, you better do the talking yourself. (For Evelina Thumboo it was different-lah. She was so young when her husband was taken, the two having been married a few days only. Poor thing, ya? That one. Her husband was killed by a tourist, you know, driving drunk on the wrong side of the road. Up in Cameron Highlands-lah, during their honeymoon, imagine. So it was easier for her to gain sympathy.)

Let me tell you, from the very beginning, I tried not to get involved. (Rose doesn't believe this. I don't know why she thinks I'm always the ringleader. Just because I'm the type to voice my thoughts, which partly used to be for her benefit only. I wanted to set her an example-lah. And yet, see now. How is it possible for your own daughter to turn out so different? If I think about this for the rest of my life, I still won't know.) So anyway, I can't remember who first mentioned it to me, but as I was saying, it was either Siew Chin or Bernadette. Dorothy, her feelings were more like mine. Poor Valerie, the fellow just died, bukan? Not even cold in the grave. No matter whether your marriage was perfect or not, you're still going to miss your husband. "How can someone be sick so long, and all our doctors can't find out why?" That's what everyone was wondering, even though, of course, no one told Valerie this to her face. But she must have sensed something-lah. True, I wondered about it myself, and to be honest, the only thing that stopped me from believing it totally was this. Okay, say maybe someone, not necessarily Valerie, but someone was doing black magic on Benjamin Nair. With all those nuns around him, how could the magic still keep working? Look how it's written in the Gospel, whenever two or three are gathered in my name, there I will be among them. And definitely more than two or three were gathered in Mount Alvernia, the whole time Benjamin Nair lay there dying.

It had to be his fate-lah. Right or not?

• • •

ANYWAY, THAT BERNADETTE. One minute she was saying everything was just my imagination, next minute, she herself was inventing stories. She was the one to ask, "Why you think the daughter didn't come home for the funeral?" just before we reached Valerie's house.

As if off-hand I would know what funeral she was talking about. Of course I knew, but what I mean is, listen to how she talked, that Bernadette. Obviously the fellow had been on her mind a while. Still waters run deep, ya?

"We know it wasn't the money," she said.

"Why not?" I said. "Could be it was the money. You know how expensive it is to fly? Especially if only for just a few days."

"Ya, but she can come home now, she couldn't come home then? And what's more important than your own father's funeral?"

"Alamak, please. That girl was over there one whole year already, you expect her to think like that?" Not that I was condoning Shakilah's behavior, okay? But I couldn't resist giving Bernadette a hard time. Every now and then, for some reason, she would rub me the wrong way, but our clashes were not serious-lah, as I've said.

"One year can't compare to your whole childhood, okay?" she said. "That wasn't the reason. It was something else."

Actually, I agreed. One year couldn't have been enough to undo eighteen years of upbringing, but that depends on what kind of upbringing you've had. That Valerie, with her modern ideas. I always knew she was giving her daughter too much freedom. That girl used to come and go as she pleased. Even on weeknights, I don't think Valerie ever gave her a curfew. No wonder the family doesn't come first with her. It's all in the upbringing.

So I said this to Bernadette, but of course, she with her one-track mind, she still insisted on another reason. So I decided, give her a chance to speak-lah.

"Okay, you so smart, what other reason can you think of?" I asked.

"That's what I mean," she said. "No one knows."

All I could do was shake my head at her. "No one knows, so?" I went on asking. What kind of answer was that to give? No one knows. As if she had to tell me that.

"Someone must know, right?" she said.

But I couldn't see her point. And for the time being, I couldn't get her to explain what she meant because now, we had arrived outside Valerie's house. (To be honest, I did understand a little bit, where she was heading. You've heard that story about a diamond woman, right? Ah, that one, I won't repeat-lah, it's so common already. Not that Bernadette and I ever talked about it anymore, and nor did Dorothy or Siew Chin, and till today, I still think it could be that music teacher from St. Agnes. You know who I mean. But anyway, most people wondered if it was Valerie. Bernadette also. And Bernadette wasn't stupid, you know. In fact, she could have gone far, if not for her health. Or then again, maybe not. I don't think she was ever that ambitious-lah, even though her exam marks used to be quite high, especially in science. Ask anyone about the rabbit she dissected in biology lab. She did it so perfectly and all by herself because her partner was absent that day. Who would have thought her capable? See how you can never tell about people.)

Ah, so anyway, Valerie must have been looking out of her window at the same time that we were reaching the house. Or maybe she was sitting there the whole time, watching the road. Could be, who knows. In that case, could be she saw something we hadn't seen, when the light changed. That was what I was thinking when her front door opened. Bernadette, she had her hand raised and she was just about to press the bell-button, and she said, "Eh?" as if so surprised. What's so surprising? Live by yourself, what else is there to do except sit by the window and watch the world go by? That's not my choice, but Valerie, as I was saying, she preferred to be left alone.

"Hello," she said, nodding her head as if welcoming us. You could tell she wasn't sure what we were doing there, okay? The doubtfulness was there in her eyes. She was afraid we were being busybodies, coming to kachau only. Ya-lah, I was aware of our reputation-lah. But what to do about that? You can't stop people from thinking what they want to think-lah. Okay, yes, you can, but to a certain limit only.

Ah, so ya-lah, I was going to start off slow, ask questions like, "How are you?" and "How's your daughter's visit coming along?" But that coconut-head friend of mine, betul-betul a coconut-head. Before I could say one word, she was already blurting out, "Eh, did you see anything just now? You saw, right? The blackout? You saw or not?"

Now Valerie was totally on guard. Of course she knew what Bernadette was talking about. How could she not know? The whole world disappearing like that, in the middle of the afternoon. Okay-lah, not to exaggerate, so it wasn't the whole world. But anyone home at the time would have noticed the air suddenly going black, whether or not there was a suitable explanation for it. (Some people think maybe because there was a dang-ki performing in the market that afternoon, and given the rumors about how after he had gone into a trance, people could hear voices in the air, I suppose there could have been a link. Some say the voices were not speaking clearly but as if in tongues, although a few people heard the voices speaking Malay, but not modern Malay. Some old-fashioned kind-lah that no one could interpret. Ah, and those two girls were there, Jo and Susanna, Alice Wang and Regina Lim's daughters, with a bunch of their St. Agnes friends. Of course they weren't supposed to go to things like that, but being teenagers, what. No one at the market remembers the air turning dark, by the way, and nowadays some want to say maybe they imagined the voices, even. But I tell you, I'm not making anything up.)

Of course it didn't surprise me when Valerie said, "Oh, was there a blackout?" as if really, she didn't know.

"Alamak, you didn't see anything? How come?" That Bernadette. It would take her a while to believe that people were not going to willingly open their mouths about this. This wasn't the usual gossip, right? Bernadette wasn't stupid, but as I've pointed out, she wasn't that observant of human nature-lah.

Valerie just shook her head. "It must have been during my nap," she said, quite calmly. "This heat, you know. It wears me out. I must have slept through the whole thing."

You hear how she was talking? Obviously she knew what Bernadette meant. Just from the way she said, "I must have slept through the whole thing," you could tell. Ah, so anyway, I saw right through her words, but definitely, I wasn't going to share this with Bernadette.

"Ya-lah, this heat," I said, trying to play along. Also, I wanted to change the subject so that, hopefully, Valerie would relax a bit. "The weather keeps getting worse. How are you keeping up, with your daughter's visit? Must be nice to have her home? We just stopped by to chat a bit."

"Oh, I'm fine. And yes, it's nice to have her home." Valerie smiled at us as if none of us were hiding anything. But you notice, still, Bernadette and I were not being invited into the house.

"Is she home for good?" Bernadette asked, finally catching on to what I was trying to do.

"No, no, she's here on holiday." Valerie kept on smiling-lah, as if that way, her heartbreak wouldn't show or something. Of course her heart was broken. Any mother can understand this. Never mind what goes on between you and your daughter, whatever disagreements, whatever quarrels, how to bear the two of you living in different countries? Not just different countries. Separate continents. In this way I've been lucky that my Rose was never that adventurous. True, I used to try to encourage her, but it's a good thing I didn't succeed.

"Eh, you must be excited-lah, you're going to have a grandchild," Bernadette went on. See, why she must put her foot in her mouth? We all knew Shakilah didn't have a wedding ring on her finger.

"A child is always a blessing," I said quickly.

Valerie looked at me as if she was trying to decide whether or not I was serious. Needless to say, she wasn't smiling anymore, okay? Actually, even I couldn't read her facial expression now.

"Yes, always," I went on. I was nodding my head and so was Bernadette. She must have realized her mistake-lah, because the next second, I heard her say, "Yes, every child, no matter what. Every child is a blessing."

"Yes," Valerie said, finally. "I think so, too." Definitely, she was not going to invite us in, thanks to Bernadette.

So that's why-lah that afternoon, despite my good intentions, I ended up not getting a chance to remind Valerie about Pontianak. The mood was ruined-lah. Besides, there was still a bit of time, I thought. We all knew the baby wasn't due for a few months. At least three months, but probably four, depending on whether it was a small baby or not. Better postpone the conversation to another day, I decided. And better not involve Bernadette the next time. That part was my mistake.

We didn't stay long after that. No point, bukan?

SO ANYWAY, BERNADETTE and I parted ways around five o'clock, give or take a few minutes. Supposedly that's when the old man was spotted again, I know. But you've heard the rumors, so you should understand. Not all the stories coincide, ya? For instance, according to one story, the chap was dressed like a World War II Japanese soldier, except he didn't have a bayonet. That's why some people started saying he could be a spirit left here to do penance-lah, for sins committed during the Occupation.

"Maybe he was the one who tied a seven-year-old girl to a rambutan tree. You remember that story?"

"You mean Mrs. Kathigasu's daughter? That was Yamashita who gave the orders-lah."

"Ya-lah, but some lowly soldier was sent to light the fire under the girl's legs, right? Maybe this was the chap. Could be-ah?"

"What about those other soldiers who participated in the massacres? Could be one of them also."

"Oh, ya-ah?"

"Eh, how come these soldiers when they appear never have blood on their uniforms? That's what I want to know."

You see how conversations eventually went off track? And in another story, can you believe? The fellow was wearing a business suit! Hiding behind the sago in the graveyard, dressed in a business suit! Betul-betul gila. Why would a ghost wearing a suit be gallivanting about in the graveyard?

"Dia was watching-lah."

"Watching what?"

"T'ak tahu-lah what he was looking for, but he could have been spying on us anyway, right?"

"Maybe he wasn't a ghost. Maybe he was a dirty old man."

"Ya-ah, maybe-ah? Alamak."

That's two versions of the story only. Other so-called witnesses couldn't even remember whether the fellow was a man or a woman. Can you believe? In this third version, there was some speculation that it could be the same lady that the bus drivers used to see, you know that old story. The one about how after midnight, sometimes there would be one old lady waiting at the bus stop outside the graveyard.

But she hadn't been seen in years, okay? (Of course every bus driver knew not to stop to pick her up. Some didn't even dare to look in the rearview mirror, not wanting to see that there was no one there.)

No use asking Bernadette about this. She's already said she saw nothing. And I can tell you, she was already on her way home, so no wonder. Supposedly, the fellow was hiding in the trees almost directly across from Ying Ying Coleman's house. You know that's not where Bernadette's house is. No need to ask her again-lah.

ASK GOPAL DHARMA, if you can catch him on one of his better days. He was the first one to tell me. I was taking out the rubbish bag that night, and he happened to be outside. He was watering his fruit trees, since he didn't do it in the morning. (Rose still doesn't know he once proposed to me, okay? Me, imagine. It's true. Gopal Dharma proposed to me, back when he and I were both still young. My Hock Siew wasn't in the picture, yet. That's how long ago I mean. Of course, it shocked me when he did it. Nowadays, intermarriages are more common, but in those days? Can you imagine? And we were not really boyfriend and girlfriend, okay? Don't ask Gopal about this. He'll tell you something different, but I never saw it that way. It was a bit awkward-lah, when Hock Siew and I got married, and then when Gopal bought the house right next door to us, I thought, Alamak, now what? But it turned out to be nothing, okay? Maybe that was the only house available at the time-lah, for the price he could afford. I mean, in this area. I can understand trying to stay in this neighborhood. We grew up around here, bukan? That's why Hock Siew and I bought this house. I didn't feel like moving to another area, and my Hock Siew, he loved me so much, even though he himself wasn't from around here, he let me have my way.)

"Good evening, Helena," Gopal started off. He was always formal like that.

"Good evening," I responded. I didn't stop, okay? But when I reached the dustbin, I heard him ask, "How are you feeling?" and his tone of concern was what made me pause-lah. So I didn't answer right away, because I was wondering why he was asking me that.

"I saw you this morning," he went on. "In the market. You didn't see me waving to you?"

"No, I didn't see you," I said to him, over my shoulder. I had no idea what he was talking about, okay? But over the years, I had made it a habit not to linger-lah, where he was concerned. Don't tempt fate, bukan? So I just put the rubbish bag in the dustbin and closed the lid, and then I was going to walk straight back into the house.

"I was going to ask if you wanted a lift home, but you disappeared so fast."

"Oh," I said, as I turned around. No need to be rude-lah, so I smiled at him through the fence. "Thanks, but that's my morning exercise, you know." Could be, that was a mistake, because of course, he smiled back.

"Oh, then I would have asked if I could walk with you, just to share your company," he said.

Can you imagine? Flirting with one old hag like me? Of course, my heart leapt a bit, but a bit only, and that's the truth. What to do? You take a man, you take a woman, what can you expect? You see how handsome Gopal Dharma is, even today? Imagine when we were young. I mean, before everything else. I tell you, in his heyday, he was more dashing than that boy Ivan, okay? So why didn't I go for him? That's what you want to know-lah. Looks aren't everything. Who can live on love and fresh air only? I'm not saying I was ever in love with him. As I've already said, we were not boyfriend and girlfriend. Passion and love are not the same thing, you know. And I never regretted marrying my Hock Siew, okay? Never.

"You seemed a bit worried, this morning," Gopal went on. "Were you worried about something?" He was finished with his watering, you know, and now he was rolling up the hose and hanging it over the tap at the side of his house. That's why I thought it was okay-lah for me to chitchat a bit. Because surely, there were other things he had to do, his pupils' homework to mark, all that. So I thought for sure we would end up talking for a few minutes only.

"No-lah, I wasn't really worried," I said. "Just the heat." Of course, I wasn't going to bring up the topic of Auntie Coco's sister with him, whether or not he knew anything about it. Winifred Teo didn't say anything about him being outside, and neither did Bernadette.

"Yes, it's getting worse," he said. He didn't come over to the fence, okay? Instead, he was walking to his front door, and then, he stood there a while, with one foot on the cement step, as if he couldn't decide-lah whether to go inside or not. I myself was at my own front door already.

"Good-night," I said. Obviously, both of us were ready to go inside, even though he was hesitating a bit.

"Good-night," he said. But he didn't move, okay?

"Is there something you want to ask me?" Don't ask why I said that. Until today, I still don't know.

Of course, he looked at me quite strangely. He wasn't expecting me to ask him that, bukan? And my heart, I tell you. Flapping here and there, like a wild hen waking up and finding itself in a cage. Ah, but luckily he didn't ask what I thought he was going to ask. He just said, "Did you hear about that old chap people around here have been seeing?"

"What old chap?" I said, because remember, I hadn't heard about the fellow yet at the time.

"The beggar in the graveyard. Be careful when you go out alone, you know? I think the children saw him first. They're always taking that short cut. You haven't heard? It seems he was seen again this afternoon."

Don't ask how Gopal could have managed to find out before me. I was wondering about this myself. "This afternoon, when?" I asked him. (Don't get me wrong. We didn't chat like this as a habit, okay? What I mean is, first of all, Gopal was not a gossipper. Second, as I've said, usually, I wouldn't linger around him.)

"Oh, around five, between five and six, something like that. That's what I've heard. It seems he was hiding behind the trees, but people saw him from their windows. It must be the same chap. Probably some harmless vagabond, I suppose, but just to be safe, I've reported it to the police. I don't know if they're going to do anything."

Do what? Definitely, I couldn't imagine our police spending their time searching the graveyard for one old beggar. But of course I didn't say so out loud. I just asked, "Which children saw him?"

But that, Gopal didn't know. He said he had heard about it only. I'm sure he was surprised I didn't know anything, but of course, he had enough tact not to show it. Ah, so anyway, that's all we said to each other. Nothing personal, okay?

So that's how I found out about the fellow-lah. Of course, later when Rose came home and then, finally, I got a chance to talk to her, I asked her about him also. But as it turned out, she also hadn't heard anything. You see-lah how hard it was to put two and two together. Right or not?

WHISPERS
FROM A FRIDAY
REVISITED

ROHANA BINTE AZIZ

daughter of aziz bin osman and aliyah binte kadir

mother deceased

sister of bettina

WHEN THE FIRST breeze came, rushing through the lalang like a thief running, touching inside me like stiff lace, here and here and here, that was when I knew. Chilly air in my head, even though Che' Halimah had prepared me to see the lady. "This time she will come with angels, tahu. Don't run when you feel the cold air." But I was afraid. At first I thought, how not to get up and run, even though Che' Halimah had advised me not to do that? My heart banging when the long grass started moving, scraping in the dark like the sharp blades of parangs. But Che' Halimah, she needed at least four of the star flowers. "No, don't dig them up before the sun goes down.

Otherwise, the flowers will rot." They were the last things on the list, and after one whole week of looking for all the plants she needed, finally, I would be done.

So I made myself stay.

Like a thief running, like hands and feet burrowing through the long sharp stalks, that breeze came, over there to my left while I was digging. I could see the lalang dancing, to and fro near the wall of the yellow shrine, the one where long time ago, Che' Halimah was telling Bettina to bury the baby.

Above my head, leaves blocking away the sky, blackest black like burnt paper, and everywhere, the milky sweetness of the bunga kubur. Frangipani, Abdul would say, with his perfect English pronunciation. My brother Abdul, his English getting better and better.

And Bapa also was getting better, able to sit up in the hospital bed already.

So I continued digging, to pay what I owed, while the lalang swayed and shook, over where the lady came through.

"AT YOUR SERVICE." Those were his first words, the one who stayed, his voice like warm rain. I hadn't been watching. I was kneeling there, concentrating on loosening the star flowers slowly so as not to break their roots, and suddenly he was behind me. Suddenly, I was turning, my banging heart turning against my will. The black leaves crumpling the sky, the lalang rumbling like sea waves along the shore, while his voice fell on my neck, turning me.

So old his face was. It was the first thing I noticed, and then I saw the petals floating between us. Blue petals with brown streaks, and yellow petals, and red petals. Then I saw a bowl, where someone's hand was dipping in. She had painted fingernails, and one diamond wedding ring.

"Do you remember me?" he asked. And the bowl and the petals, they disappeared.

Che' Halimah had said to me, "Don't be afraid of the lady," but nothing about, "One of them will speak to you." Nothing about what to say.

"Don't be afraid," he said.

And then I was not afraid. His voice between us like wind carrying sunlight, like a door flying open. Him the one doing magic on me, so I tried to turn my face away.

"There's no need to be afraid."

Something was breathing in his hands, breathing like a bud, its shadow too small to see, but you could feel it. And the lalang was still shaking, over there by the yellow shrine, but the others all gone through now.

Why was he speaking to me? I wondered. And Che' Halimah, why had she not warned me?

"Do you remember? You were fifteen years old. You wore a blue dress."

His words cracking me open, reaching inside me like a hand. Then it was too much. The last thing I saw was him leaning towards me, his body burning, his face flickering against the sky. Black leaves blowing everywhere.

ABDUL WAS THE one who came looking for me, his voice the first thing I heard when I was waking up. Calling to me, "Kechil, where are you? Kechil!" Sending my name over the ground, sending it to me like his own breath. My name, this nickname they used to call me, because before Abdul was born, I had been the youngest: Kechil. Abdul's voice was already changing, and I could hear he sounded just like Mahmud when he called to me. And the thought beat like a stick against my heart, making one spreading blue-black bruise.

Maybe his voice was the thing that had woken me, calling again and again, "Kechil!" until I was able to open my eyes.

There was something stuck to the branch directly overhead,

one torn, dead piece, like something shrivelled up. Around it, the leaves were ticking, and a bit of light shone out just behind, between that branch and the sky. Then one last breeze passed through, going through my bones. And it was over.

And I saw Abdul, standing in the lalang, with his friend Matthew, that Eurasian boy with the Chinese mother, the one with his father always yelling at him. That one. He also was there that night.

"Kechil!" Abdul's voice was afraid, when he came running.

"Kenapa sini?" I asked him, when he bent down to help me. His arms still thin like a boy's arms, but becoming strong, I could feel. One hand underneath my left wrist, his other hand on my right elbow, he helped me to balance myself as I stood up.

"Why are you here?" he said, repeating my question to me.

His friend Matthew walked over, a hush following him in the darkness. Always, I could hear that boy's footsteps tender on the ground.

"And what are these for?" Abdul asked, when he noticed my basket with the star flowers. "You came here just to collect these things?"

"What time is it?" I asked him. How come Che' Halimah had not come looking for me? She was the only one who knew exactly where I was.

"Almost midnight," Abdul said, and he asked again, "So, eh, what are the flowers for?"

"For cooking-lah," I said. "How long did you look for me?"

"Maybe half-an-hour or so." Abdul turned to check with his friend, who was kneeling beside the basket now. "Right?"

Matthew nodded. He kept on looking at the flowers, some kind of yearning inside him spilling out when he smiled at me, as if there was a secret he was keeping, which he thought I knew about.

"Eh, what happened?" Abdul asked. "Did you faint or something?"

"You see anyone else or not?" I asked him, just to be sure.

"You mean here? At this hour?" Abdul shook his head at me, as if he was the elder brother. "Who else gila like you? Everyone else, when they go out for a walk, this isn't where they go for a walk, you know."

"I told you before, that's why it's safe here, ya? The only people who dare to come in here at night," I started, but he interrupted me.

"I know, I know. Because their hearts are pure, they know they have nothing to fear." He gave a huge sigh, just like Bapa when he did that. "You haven't heard about that guy? We heard about him today. Right, Matthew?"

Matthew nodded, still kneeling beside the basket.

"What guy?" I asked, my heart getting nervous.

"Some guy's been hanging around our school, and they've seen him at St. Agnes and Our Lady of Lourdes also. Some people think he's just a beggar, except he never asks for money. He likes to talk to children. Brother Dennis thinks he might be a child molester."

It was him, the angel who had stayed behind, who had done magic on me. Was it because he thought I was Bettina? She was the one, my sister, who had been wearing a blue dress when she was raped. My heart became more nervous.

"The teachers haven't seen him." Matthew was speaking now, his voice quieter than Abdul's, soft like the soil after rain.

Then Abdul took over again. "No, that's right. None of the teachers have seen him. They say at the girls' schools, the teachers haven't seen him, either."

"He only appears to children," whispered Matthew, dipping his hand into the basket.

"You better watch out for him," Abdul said, while I was thinking how to make them go home without me. More than ever now, I must bring Che' Halimah her flowers, I thought, so that after that, my part would be finished. Whatever was going on, I didn't want to join in.

Matthew was running his fingers through the flowers, and that was when I saw. There were more than two of the star flowers. More even than four. The basket was full.

"WHY YOU DIDN'T come to look for me?" I asked Che' Halimah, when I got there. As soon as she opened the door, I couldn't stop myself, my mouth opening like your dress hem coming loose. "Why you just left me alone? You didn't worry what was happening to me?"

"I didn't leave you alone." Her voice calm as the night itself, quiet as the night was now. Quiet as if her words were not words. As if her words leaves and grass, her words the fragrant air, the rain coming that we could smell.

Behind her, shadows darted around the room, but at first, I saw nobody there. A red candle was burning on Che' Halimah's kitchen table. Next to the candle, there were some pieces of yellow cloth, and a wooden bowl like the bowl I had seen with the oil in it, but this one was empty.

"You didn't worry?" I asked her, although my heart whispered to itself, Kechil, how you dare speak to Che' Halimah like that? And yet, my tongue couldn't stop. "And you didn't tell me everything. You didn't warn me."

Che' Halimah looked past my head as if Abdul and Matthew were outside, but I knew they were not there. I had left them sleeping at home, Matthew staying over in Abdul's room like sometimes he would. I had made sure they were both asleep, before I had come over again. My brother was still a boy in the end, never mind his grown-up ways.

Then she looked at me, her face in the darkness as if itself a shadow, only her eyes clear and shining. "You are okay now?" she asked me. Her voice tender because she knew. "Your father is okay now?"

"Yes," I said. "The fever is gone."

Che' Halimah, she knew I could see the shadows. "Mahu masok, t'ak?" she asked.

Quiet her voice, tender her voice, but I didn't want to go in. I was becoming afraid again. Whatever Che' Halimah was doing, I didn't want to know. So I gave her the basket, with no explanation about how it had become so full of the star flowers. I told her only, "I must go home," hoping she would think because it was so late, already after midnight, as if she couldn't feel my fear.

"Okay," she said. "Go before the rain comes. Otherwise, you'll get wet."

And that was all.

But as I was turning away, I smelled bunga kubur drifting from across the room. And then I saw he was there, bending in the corner between the oven and the corridor that took you to Che' Halimah's bedroom. Definitely it was him. One moment human, another moment whoosh! Only black leaves swirling in the candlelight. He was looking at something on the ground, something at his feet, and his right hand was holding up a kris. I saw the silver blade flash in the candlelight.

And in the corridor, there was someone else. Someone whispered *Jibrail, Jibrail*, when he swung back his arm, the kris rising in the darkness. Then he let go and it dropped straight down, and I saw on the ground a round, hard fruit, almost like a coconut. I saw the kris fall into it, and the shell split open, and light burst out, suddenly like that, bathing the air. I knew if I looked up, I would see the face of whoever was in the corridor, but I didn't look in that direction.

Che' Halimah, she was watching me as I turned my face away, watching me as I went down her front steps. She knew I had seen what I did not wish to see. I could feel her hand as if it was on my back, stroking me.

Then I heard the door close. Then I wondered, how had I known that was a kris he was holding? How come I had been able to see what was on the ground, at his feet?

I could hear the voice, speaking as if not from inside the house, as if coming from the air itself. Someone was asking, "Like this?" The one in the corridor. I knew it must be her.

Che' Halimah was saying, "No, slowly. Arrange carefully. Take your time."

"Like this?" the one in the corridor asked again. I could hear she was young, maybe only a few years older than Abdul.

"Slower."

Jibrail—Gabriel, you would say—he was silent. Him the witness and the messenger. This knowledge came to me like something spoken, but not within my understanding. Only Mahmud used to understand things like that, everyone saying Mahmud had magic in him. He would touch the soil, and watch how the roots of trees were growing, in which directions. Whenever you couldn't find him at home, you knew he was in the graveyard. Sitting underneath a tree, studying the leaves when they floated down. Why he did not have enough magic to save himself when the thieves came? Not enough to save Kadir, Noi, Bettina. Only me and Abdul. Only us two were left, and Bapa, because Mahmud had told me to go with Bapa when Bapa went out to the shop that night, and to take Abdul along.

Abdul was the one to hope in now. Day after day I would tell myself, concentrate on Abdul.

That night I still didn't know, what had happened to me.

"Will they come back?" the one in the corridor was asking.

"One of them will come back."

"This one. It's this one, ya?"

"Betul. Good. And the other one?"

"The other one . . . "

"Not the boy."

"The other one . . . I can't see her."

"Slowly."

"Where's the other one?"

"Slowly. Don't move your hand so fast. See, your arrangement is not right. Concentrate."

Quiet, Che' Halimah's voice. Patient like the angels.

"Who's that?"

"Look closely. Look again."

"This one will die."

"And the baby?"

"A baby will live."

"Correct. Betul. Good."

THE RAIN WAS fierce when it came, the sky loose as if the universe was fighting, as if everywhere trees were bursting open, as if petals were exploding, the wind slashing the bunga kubur to shreds. Birds were screaming in the leaves, and while the water poured down, the air smelled like blood, as if somewhere nearby, blood was dripping through the night.

After that, it was over. That Saturday morning at sunrise, there was not a sign left.

Abdul, he was so protected, the rain didn't wake him. Bapa also, when we went to see him in the hospital, he wondered how come he had slept through a thunderstorm like that. All the nurses were chattering about it, he said. Only I had been awake. I the only witness in our kampong.

Now you.

LULU MENDEZ

MALIKA COULDN'T REMEMBER most of what she had been dreaming about as she roused herself out of the cane armchair to answer the phone, which had been ringing for some time in the living room. (Malika had heard it while asleep, an ambiguous melody forming in the distance.) There had been a river in her dream, a glistening expanse of iridescent water, vibrant with slippery shapes beneath the surface. Malika could still hear a voice calling to her from the riverbank as she groped her way around the door jamb and towards Madam's rosewood stand. (She hadn't noticed yet that the bulb in the patio lamp had blown its fuse, nor was Malika aware of the book in her lap slipping to the floor when she had stood up, so concentrated were her efforts on recovering the details of her dream before she was fully awake and lost them.) She couldn't be sure as the voice faded if it had been a man's or a woman's, or a child's. What she had heard, first, was a flurry of leaves, and then that voice fanning out over the water like praises to Allah broadcast from one of the old mosques in the evening. (Sali would ask if it could have belonged to the man in the songkok but Malika would say no, something about this dream had felt different to her. It didn't have the ambiance of her old recurring nightmares.)

Madam's rosewood stand was underneath the window with the mango tree outside. It was hand-carved (found in the same shop in which Madam had bought her jewelry boxes), with slim notched legs to resemble bamboo, and three square shelves. Phone books sat on the bottom shelf, the phone was on the middle shelf, and on the top shelf was a miniature jade tree (freed, like the Italian sculptor Michelangelo's angels, from a rock of pink jade), its opalescent leaves upturned as if surrounded by rushing wind. (Madam used to keep the tree wrapped in brown paper and stored in a cupboard in her bedroom, to protect it while the children were growing up, but in 1982, while Malika was helping Madam clean out various cupboards around the house on the weekend that Michelle was leaving for Australia, the tree had been taken out and set on the rosewood stand as a temporary measure—"Just till I can find the right home for it," Madam had said. Michelle's husband had just been transferred by the textile company for which he worked to Perth, and Madam and Malika had had only had a few months to get used to the idea. On that weekend, the thought that none of the children was likely ever to live in Singapore again had exploded with such ferocity in both of their hearts, only the most mundane and repetitive of tasks were manageable. Malika would remember how before it had occurred to Madam to clean out the cupboards, the two of them had dusted and polished all of the furniture and mopped the floor in every room. Even the windows and sliding doors had been washed, Madam getting down on her knees and scrubbing the steel grooves with the mindful attention of a servant. She, Malika, couldn't explain why the jade tree was still on the stand, where it had since lost six and a half leaves, the tip of the seventh most recently. This last one had been broken by the youngest of Michelle's girls, Nicole, who had started learning to walk last December. Caroline's and Francesca's boys had each had his turn when they were Nicole's age, all except for the eldest, Brendan, the gentle and musically minded one, the one Madam would not admit was her favorite).

She fingered the jagged nub left by one of the missing leaves as she lifted the receiver with her other hand.

"Malika?"

It was Madam, sounding worried. Malika glanced over her shoulder at the clock and saw it was half-past nine. "Yes, Madam, everything's okay at home," she said promptly. "Sorry, Madam, I fell asleep while reading."

"Alamak, you. Gave me quite a scare, you know."

Malika could hear in the background the papery rush of wind through treetops and a scattering of leaves on a hard surface (perhaps a cement pavement or the tarmac of a car park). "Sorry, Madam," she said again, wondering where Madam was and what had led Madam finally to use the hand phone Caroline had given to her at Christmas, which Caroline had programmed so that her own hand phone number, Francesca's and Michelle's, and Madam's home phone number could each be dialed with a single press of a button. Madam had been carrying the phone around in her handbag, insisting she didn't know how to use it—"One can't teach an old dog new tricks," Malika would hear her say, whenever the topic of computers arose, particularly the topic of the government's mandating the use of computers in the school curriculum. (It was Caroline who was paying Singapore Telecoms directly for global service on Madam's phone, afraid that if she left it up to her mother, Madam would willfully let the account lapse.)

Madam didn't tell Malika where she was or whether she had been driving around all the while. What she told Malika was that she was going to stop at the Newton hawker center for a bowl of tau suan. She had called to ask if Malika would like some tau suan or another kind of dessert (as Malika had several favorite desserts and one couldn't easily guess at what she might have a taste for, and Madam would know this, having had Malika in her house since Malika was twelve).

Malika imagined the sweet, glutinous lentils sticking to her palate, too sweet for what she wanted on this night. She pondered her other options (knowing all the stalls at Newton well, where each stall was situated and which might be closed due to an illness or a family vacation). A slice of tapioca cake? She wouldn't have minded a slice of tapioca cake, but as her favorite nyonya stall was nowhere near Madam's favorite tau suan stall, Malika settled on pulot hitam from a stall just down the aisle from the latter. She realized as she gave Madam her answer that she would have preferred tapioca cake to the sweet rice, craving suddenly the aftertaste of coconut milk when baked, but then what she wanted more than a savory comfort was for Madam not to weave her way around more tables than was necessary, traipse past all those hungry eyes, listen to the carnivorous longing manifested in sighs and low whistles (although from what I've heard and to which Malika would agree eventually, Madam herself didn't appear flustered by the men, so accustomed was she to their intrusive stares, to their cheap gestures of desire in the fluorescent public light—boys had been following Madam home from school and whistling at her from hawker tables along the Malaccan roadside ever since she was a young girl, when her breasts were only just starting to grow and she was wearing basic cotton bras of the market variety, size 28, three for fifteen cents).

"Malika, if you're tired, don't wait up for me-ah?" Madam was saying. "I'll put the pulot hitam in the fridge and it'll be there for your breakfast. Okay?"

When Madam hung up, the click at the end of the line was so quiet, Malika almost missed it. She listened for a moment longer, then put the receiver back in its cradle.

Beyond the lower branches of the mango tree caught in a splash of light from the living room windows, Madam's garden was a sea of black and gray leaves (Malika's own words when later she described the darkness outside). There was a stillness to the air interrupted only by the slender shimmer of the white posts of the car porch, and a glint of fencing at the edge along the hibiscus bushes of the family next-door. (Malika thought she could see the umbrella tops of the family's papaya trees as well, but she wasn't sure if this was only because she knew the trees were there.) Nothing was moving in the sugar cane, not a frog or a snail or the tremor of a breeze. The British gentleman's house over the wall on the other side of Madam's garden was silent, as were all of the neighboring houses, and even the insects seemed asleep in the grass.

It was then that Malika recalled her earlier sense of foreboding (realizing at the same time that the patio lamp was out, she was turning away from the windows to get a new bulb from the storage cabinet in the kitchen when she noticed the upper windows in the next-door family's house, and the head of one of the children leaning over a windowsill—Malika wasn't sure which child it was, but when she thought about it later, she would wonder if something in the child's posture had hinted to her it was the daughter, who must have climbed onto a chair to look out at something in the garden. But at what was anyone's guess, as all Malika could hear when she looked back upon this night was its soundlessness, and a soft trickle of rain, peculiar only because the rain would fall elsewhere on the island, miles away in the vicinity of Miss Shakilah's neighborhood, where Sali and I were).

Malika switched on the light in the corridor and made her way towards the kitchen, past the photographs of Madam's grandchildren on the walls. (Some had been taken during their visits to Singapore, a few when Madam had gone to visit them, always without Malika because much of the family's savings had been depleted by Madam's husband's illness and because visas to Western countries were hard to get for someone suspected of travelling as an employee, which was why the photographs of Madam's trips were for Malika inexplicably painful and pleasurable, as on the one hand she missed how things used to be, when Madam had taken her on all of the family's vacations—to Cameron Highlands, Bali, Sydney—and on the other hand Malika missed the children, both Madam's daughters and the grandchildren. She missed seeing and hearing them wandering about the house, sweat gleaming off their faces like the shine off freshwater pearls).

She paused as she often did at the last of the photographs, which showed Madam and Brendan laughing into the camera on their way to Sentosa Island in September of 1978 (the year Brendan was three and Francesca had flown home after only eight months in London, armed with complaints about the lack of spice in English food, which Malika hadn't doubted had been one of Francesca's reasons for coming home for a visit so soon, but as Madam had suspected as well—she had confessed as much to Malika—it probably hadn't been the only reason).

One could almost hear Madam laughing in the photograph as she pressed her face into Brendan's curls and sniffed at the salt and sunshine in his hair. It had been a windy day. There were waves in the water and Malika could feel the tickling of the wind through the collar of Brendan's blue-and-white-striped T-shirt. She could feel Madam's happiness, absolute and full, as if that visit of Francesca's hadn't been at all worrisome for her, which Malika knew wasn't so. (It had been completely out of character for Francesca to leave her job, even temporarily, more so for her to stay with her parents for two months. When asked how it was that her husband didn't mind, Francesca had replied airily that as Gareth had been promoted recently and was overwhelmed with new responsibilities at his father's law firm, he had welcomed the opportunity not to have the children underfoot for a while— Brendan wasn't much of a problem, but Bryce at eighteen months was prone to throwing tantrums. "Gareth's not used to living in the same house as someone with a temper," Malika would remember Francesca's saying to Madam. Both she and Madam had intuited that Francesca was referring to her father, in his healthier days. Everyone in the family had been used to him.)

Malika didn't know if Madam had ever asked Francesca directly if there was turmoil brewing in her marriage. (Francesca's other visits home weren't clouded in the same way. She would never again return for more than a week's holiday, although the boys would sometimes stay a month. Whatever marital distress there was appeared to have dissipated over time, and the topic had not arisen since. If there was anyone who knew for sure, it would be Caroline or Michelle, but the sisters were loyal and Malika knew one would never betray another's confidence.)

A breeze lifted the hem of the window curtain above the sink as she stepped past the photograph of Madam and Brendan and entered the kitchen (before her hand touched the light switch). Malika saw the ashy white lace shudder like a naked shoulder across the room. She would speak later of the impression she had had of moonlight grazing a collarbone, and of a scar nestled at the base of a throat, a tiny white scar shaped like a clipped cuticle. Then her thumb had hit the switch and the fluorescent light came on, and Malika could not determine if she had only imagined there had been someone in the room. (And so there would always be loose ends when she talked about this night. Even the shape of the scar was a loose end, as when Sali asked, "Why compare it to a clipped cuticle, Malika? Why not use something more poetic, like a crescent moon or something," all Malika could do was shake her head and caress her red bead, smiling inwardly at the endless fraying of clarity. Was it simply her imagination or was there some truth to the somewhat vision- ary texture of the moment? Was enlightenment possible only if one endured fracture and incompleteness of meaning?)

Of course such thoughts would occur to Malika only later. As the kitchen light flooded the room she reminded herself visions were bestowed only upon saints or poets (of any reli- gion, and only later would it occur to us to wonder if when Westerners spoke of visions, sometimes they had seen ghosts). Malika stepped towards the storage cabinet, flipped open the pale oak door, took out the box of light bulbs, and plucked one from its cardboard pocket. As she set the box back on the upper shelf of the cabinet, she sensed again a chilling foreboding, this time like the blunt tip of a knife against her tailbone. Malika could feel then the existence of a common world between the girl in the sugar cane and the shoulder, the collarbone, the throat and the scar. But as she was neither poet nor saint, for months (until the birth of Miss Shakilah's baby), Malika would ascribe these sensations to her imagination, overflowing wave upon wave like the heartache in Madam's house.

She closed the door of the cabinet, switched off the kitchen light and as she left the room, a lizard crossed the floor behind her, flicking its quick, small tongue.

SOMETIMES THE MAN wearing the songkok would visit Malika only for a minute. At those times he wouldn't enter the room, but remain outside in the passageway, his scent stealing across her floor from the crack underneath the door (a syrupy blend of rose oil, sandalwood, and some kind of fruit). At other times Malika would open her eyes to see him standing by the win- dowsill, the bone of his arm visible through his sleeve as he rest- ed his hand (always his left hand) palm down on the narrow ledge. (When the moon was full the massive shadows of the flamboyant trees would waver against the translucent glass, the separate branches indistinguishable at this hour. On the floor by Malika's bed the moonlight would fall in a broken square as it passed over the top of the man's songkok, grazing the tip of his shoulder and the line of his arm. Malika would remember these facts in plodding fashion when the day arrived on which she began to doubt the rationale of boundaries prescribed between truth and imagination (Miss Shakilah's words to Madam during another of their conversations). She would wonder then (as she would remember Miss Shakilah wondering) if beyond one's cognitive senses there was a door swinging back and forth between the two, if truth was a cave within what one perceived to be merely a memory, or a nightmare or a dream, or a fantasy inspired by a library book. The flamboyant trees looming outside her window, the cut of moonlight on her floor, the tilt of the man's songkok and the angle of his arm, even the way the cuff of his sleeve touched the windowsill—they would return to her with a significance inarticulable to anyone else, but from what we could see, it brought her moments of peace and in the end that would have to be enough.)

On the nights that Malika didn't dream herself awake and the man climbed onto her bed, she would feel his knees and elbows clambering over her as if he were a child or an animal, unequipped with the smooth and satiny touch one expected of a lover. The first few times he had used his finger and as Malika was sixteen and easily moistened by hormonal stirrings, it hadn't hurt very much when she had felt her vagina pried open (after some fumbling with her labia). There had been a slight sting when the man's fingernail had scraped her hymen (Malika was sure she had heard a pop when the membrane broke), and then it was over. Intercourse would be painful at first, but after a while Malika found herself growing accustomed to it and then her skin no longer smarted and her pelvis no longer ached.

family had packed up and left or perhaps had never arrived. She gazed into the stillness of the surrounding foliage, the jagged outlines and untamed crests of treetops looming out of the gardens of Madam's other neighbors, and before she turned away and told herself that old age was starting to creep up on her, a hand brushed past Malika's upper arm. Her heart skipped a beat as someone breathed into her ear.

It wasn't the quick hot breath of a child but the slower, wearier breath of someone much older, and Malika would remember hearing a small gasp as she pulled the sliding door shut (but perhaps it was herself she was hearing, she would wonder aloud as she paused in the middle of her story) and snapped the tiny steel lock into place. She switched on the overhead patio light. A harsh white glare fell over the mosaic tiles and the furniture outside (the coffee table would have to be taken to a carpenter for reweaving soon, Malika noted as she caught sight of a curled strip hanging loosely off the bottom of one of the legs).

Through the glass of the sliding doors came the rumble of a bus on the main road. Malika sighed with relief at the ordinariness of the sound, but she would confess later that as she stepped away from the doors to start closing Madam's windows around the house, something or someone moved from the car porch onto the grass, and for a moment she felt as if a crowd were gathering in Madam's garden, and the night was webbed with souls.

Sali's point made sense, however (that if Madam's house were haunted, or sat on a haunted plot of land, this fact would have been revealed long ago) and Malika repeated it to herself as she locked the iron clasp on the window above the rosewood stand.

She did look through the glass towards the sugar cane, but the girl wasn't there. Malika was sure of this, and it would remain in the years to come a detail of which she would always be sure.

ROSE SIM

S HAK HAD HER hand on the iron bar of the doctor's gate.
I could see the emerald bracelet around her wrist, the green
stones so clear and deep, so clean, so simple. We used to share
our jewelry, you know, although mostly it was Shak's jewelry,
whatever her mother would dare to let us wear. Some would be
her grandmother's bracelets, beautiful Peranakan antique pieces
with rubies and jade set in twenty-two carat gold, I remember.
Shak, she had manipulated her mother into letting her wear
them by saying, "If you hadn't quarrelled with my grandmother, she wouldn't have kicked us out of the family." That was
how she used to be when she wanted something, even though

she knew it was because of her father that her grandmother had kicked her mother out. (Because Shak's mother had gone against Shak's grandmother's will and gotten married even after Shak's grandmother had said no. Because the grandmother was prejudiced against anyone who wasn't Chinese, especially when it came to marriage. Or so I've heard.) So Shak used to wear her grandmother's bracelets, and although I had never seen this emerald one, I assumed that was where it had come from.

"He saw us," she was saying, and when I didn't respond right away, she looked at me as if to check whether I was listening, as if I would ever not listen to her. I was the one who had remained faithful and loyal to her, no matter what. "Do you remember that night? Rose?"

Her accent was almost like that Jason fellow's, the sounds in her words flopping about, and every r chasing the air. (Not that I minded, of course. Because Shak wasn't doing it on purpose, trying to sound angmo.) I could hear her voice drifting off into the doctor's garden, familiar almost as if we were young girls again, even with her sounding American. She was still Shak to me, you know, and deep down inside, I was sure I was still Rose to her. Even if she was carrying in her watermelon womb a child everyone suspected was mixed. Even if everyone couldn't help wondering how she could manage to make love to an angmo. I especially. Maybe because I didn't want to imagine it, her fingers stroking that canary hair. That animal hair, with the pale skin underneath.

"Rose?"

A breeze was blowing about in the garden, the grass and weeds swaying at the tips, overgrown and deep. I tried to feel whether there was someone watching us, but there was only the breeze, and shadows appearing and disappearing like a dance as some afternoon clouds moved into the pathway of the sun.

Shak was almost holding her breath, I could feel it. Not desperately, but as if the world might stop spinning on its axis if she were to hear me say I didn't know what night she was referring to, which wouldn't have been the truth, but let bygones be bygones, as I've said. Why dig up what's best left buried? Although I had known from the moment she had said she wanted to see the doctor's house, what she was really talking about, I must have thought that seeing the house would be enough. Because it would confirm for her everything had existed, we had existed, on that long ago night when the doctor was dragging his son out to the gate, and we had happened to be stepping off the bus.

Whether that was what had kept her away, or brought her back, I didn't want to ask. I was afraid to ask, although I wouldn't have been able to tell you what, exactly, frightened me about it.

Just seeing the house felt enough to me. Standing there with Shak, actually looking through the gate at the dingy white walls, the red door with the brass knocker imported from overseas, the dirty windows.

For nine years already, the house had been empty, although the doctor and his wife still owned it (because they hadn't managed to sell it, for some reason). Even the brass plate with the doctor's name that used to hang on the gate was gone, and with the garden so untidy and the cement driveway littered with leaves, the property looked quite forlorn. Nothing like the way it used to look, when the doctor's servants used to take care of everything, and yet, I would avert my eyes whenever I passed it.

Life goes on, you know, and out of the blue, here we were.

"Yes, I remember." I spoke quickly before I could change my mind, and I was glad about it, because there was such relief in Shak's eyes, and the way she smiled at me, as if to say thank you.

But I didn't understand enough, you know. And the next time, I wouldn't be as brave, because I didn't understand enough.

WHAT I REMEMBER about that night. The amber porch light in the driveway, and the beautiful mandarin orange plant, still healthy, growing in the earthen pot beside the front door. (The son would pluck all the mini oranges off one morning in the future, you know. For no apparent reason, was what the amah had said when people asked. Because that was the kind of child he was, so naughty, you couldn't imagine. Not at all like his sister. His younger sister, even if only by a year. She had been a perfect child. Did the amah really believe it, or was she trying to be faithful to the doctor and his wife? For job security? Who could blame her, either way?) The front door wide open, the doctor's wife standing and watching with her arms folded across her chest. Bougainvillea petals tipping over the edges of earthen pots along the fence.

And on the other side of the fence, Laura Timmerman's house. Our classmate Laura Timmerman, who was married and living in Australia by now. But her father was still living in the house, and sometimes I would see him at the market, although his servant usually did the shopping.

And there was a niece staying with him, who went to St. Agnes. Sometimes I would see her also, she and her friends, two of whom were from our road.

WE WERE AT the doctor's gate five minutes at the most. I was keeping an eye out for anything peculiar, but all I saw were the grass and weeds moving with the breeze, and blossoms falling off the flamboyant trees to our right, healthy and fiery in the sun.

Shak was gazing towards the house, studying it as if to memorize its faded look, so as to replace the house we used to know with this one. I could feel her taking in the dried streaks of rain and dust on the walls, the locked front door and windows, the empty earthen pot with a crack in it, the other pots by the fence no longer there. I hadn't told her about the Jason fellow, or that Isabella had been at the library earlier that afternoon, partly because I was doing what Isabella was going to do, which was to leave it up to Shak to bring up the ghost, if there was a ghost involved.

And partly, even though only a few hours had passed, already my encounter with Isabella felt ancient, as if it had taken place ages ago, in a different world. (Because that was how the library was for me, you know, a very different world from our neighborhood. Modern and public, would be one way to put it. And whatever happened there felt like that, as if it really had nothing to do with what went on on our road, which wasn't true, of course.)

Shak wasn't looking at the garden, until we started smelling the rambutans that were rotting behind the house. Laura Timmerman used to tell us about the rambutan trees, not visible from the gate. The doctor's servants used to gather the fruits in brown paper bags and give at least two bags to Laura's family, the sweetest rambutans you ever tasted.

But all she said was, "I'm surprised the government's leaving the property like that." That was what she said, Shak.

And I was relieved, although perhaps also slightly disappointed. Hard to tell, now.

"Do you like it, Rose? All the changes? Only beauty allowed."

"The government doesn't own it, yet," I said, about the doctor's property, because Shak seemed to be accusing someone of something, I could hear it in her tone. Just a touch of bitterness. But was it directed at me or at the government, and what was there to accuse us of? How else was Singapore to survive without changing, staying ahead of the times? Had Shak forgotten this wasn't America? That our soil wasn't suitable for farming, even if we could afford the space? That we even had to buy our water from Malaysia?

Fifteen years couldn't have erased that much, surely. She was from here. She should know, I thought, as I watched a flamboyant blossom spiral out of the shade of the tree's branches, then waver in the sunlight before dropping into the weeds.

"I'm glad," Shak said, and when I looked at her, she was smiling. "I'm glad it hasn't been sold to them. At least, they haven't touched this part."

Her old, usual, honest smile.

"They will," I heard myself saying, suddenly. "You can bet on it. Would you believe, the government's giving free money to people who want to renovate their homes? All you have to do is promise to follow their guidelines for the renovation, to make sure your house fits in with the landscape."

"Make sure your house fits in with the landscape," Shak repeated, the breeze in the garden taking away her words like scraps of paper in the air.

"You're lucky you came home in time."

"I'm lucky." Shak smiled again, but differently now.

Perhaps because she didn't have to live here and make the best of whatever circumstances, because she wasn't the one left behind. And because she hadn't chosen to come back, and not even to write and explain to me why. (One short visit after fifteen years didn't count, not in that way, even by letting bygones be bygones.) Because hurt feelings can last a long time, and we were supposed to be closer than anyone else, and deep down inside, we were.

Perhaps because of all of that, I was saying things that jabbed and pinched her like the fingers of a spoiled brat.

I turned away and listened to the breeze settling into the weeds, embarrassed at myself.

We left soon after that, and as we were walking off, Matthew Coleman was across the road, slipping into the cemetery through the open gate. Probably taking the short cut to his house, I thought. (Because there was a raggedy path that wound around the trees and gravesites, more or less cutting diagonally across the cemetery.) I remember Shak asking, "Who's that?" She didn't know Matthew of course, although she was watching him as if she did, her eyes following the white patch of Matthew's T-shirt as he disappeared into the shrubbery, which took less than a minute, because of how overgrown everything was.

When I told her Matthew was Adelaide Coleman's younger grandson, Shak said quietly, "Doesn't he remind you of the doctor's son?" but I didn't think she could be referring to the way Matthew was always getting into trouble, since she didn't even know who he was.

So all I said was, "Boys at that age, that's how they are."

Shak didn't say anything. She was touching her womb with just the tip of her right index finger, as if afraid to let even the shadow of her hand pass over the baby's face while it slept. "You're right, Rose," she whispered, and somehow I knew she meant, what I had said about her coming home in time.

About her being lucky.

Maybe that was why she wouldn't bring up everything later, even if she wanted to.

AUNTIE COCO WAS sweeping outside her gate when we turned onto our road. Hers was the house next door to Evelina Thumboo's, so I remember what time it must have been, because Evelina Thumboo was standing underneath her jacaranda tree, watering her dead husband's ashes. She always did that, you know, at six o'clock, once a week, always on a Friday. From the time Shak and I were children, people were saying it was because her husband had been killed by a tourist driving drunk in the middle of their honeymoon. Evelina Thumboo was in so much grief, no wonder, her mind was half-gone. She had buried her husband's ashes underneath the jacaranda, and every Friday she would water them, hoping to bring him back to life. This had been going on since Shak and I were seven years old, so it was part of our childhood. Like a ritual, you know, Evelina Thumboo watering the roots of the jacaranda, we seeing her.

So it must have been around six o'clock. Evelina Thumboo smiled at us through the fence when she saw us, and I remember Shak's breath, warming my ear as she leaned towards me and whispered, "She's still doing that, huh?" as if everything was back to normal between us. As if I hadn't accused her of betrayal in some way, just a few minutes ago, outside the doctor's gate.

I smiled at her, at Shak, and nodded, glad that ours was a true friendship.

Auntie Coco's sister was sitting underneath the awning over the front door, shelling peas and looking up now and then to watch as the cemetery leaves that Auntie Coco was sweeping off the roadside floated up and into the monsoon drain. Barbara, the sister's name was, but not even Auntie Coco called her that. She was sitting in a folding chair with the basket of peas in her lap, and a yellow Tupperware bowl on the ground, at her feet. Her mouth hanging half open like always, as she watched Shak and me approach her house. It was her mouth that gave her away, you know. Because otherwise, who could tell just by look-ing, she was retarded? Auntie Coco always dressed her so nice-ly, the sister. Buying her clothes from Isetan, making sure her hair was always neatly combed. She even plucked her sister's eyebrows for her and helped her with a bit of lipstick.

"Hello, how are you?" Auntie Coco was saying to Shak, as we were about to pass her gate. Her tone was friendly, and I didn't pick up on any hidden agenda. Besides, Auntie Coco wasn't the yakkity-yak sort, you know, although she may have been curi-ous like everyone else, about the baby's father.

"Hello," said Shak, while I noticed her glancing at the sister, who was watching us now as if we were on television.

"Hello, Auntie Coco," I said, and Shak and I would have kept on walking, because there was no reason for us to stop, and also, Shak was getting tired, I could tell from the way she smiled at Auntie Coco. Because the heat was getting to her, I thought, when I saw her eyes had a wandering expression, as if she didn't have the energy to focus.

But then, Auntie Coco asked us, "Eh, Rose, eh, you and your friend stop and talk a while, can?"

So we stopped, out of politeness only.

Different from when we were outside the doctor's gate, here there was no breeze blowing about, the asphalt sloping up hot and dry. The air ticking with frogs and insects, with mosquitoes and grasshoppers mostly, although in our schooldays there used to be butterflies also, fluttering their psychedelic wings over the gravesites in the cemetery, and in Gopal Dharma's garden.

There were no other neighbors outside, as far as I could see, everyone else either preparing for dinner or not at home.

"You just came back from America-ah?" Auntie Coco was asking Shak. "Are you back for good?"

"No, just for a visit," replied Shak.

"Ah, you have a good doctor here or not?" Auntie Coco went on.

Shak hesitated for a moment, then said, "My mother's gynecologist." She looked taken aback at the question, as if in America, no one would ask this sort of thing, as if it might be considered rude.

"Ah, who?" asked Auntie Coco.

"Dr. Tay something."

"Hmm."

Shak glanced at me, and I tried to smile back reassuringly, although whether or not it worked, I wasn't sure.

"You didn't go to see him, yet, right?" Auntie Coco continued.

"No, I have an appointment."

"Ah, when?"

Shak hesitated again, then said slowly, "Monday."

Auntie Coco nodded as if to agree that Monday was the best day, or as if she had already sensed the appointment was on Monday, and now it was confirmed. She was known to be a bit clairvoyant, you know, Auntie Coco, and some people were saying she may have been born with a veil, which would mean she could see ghosts also. But why she would be clairvoyant about something like a doctor's appointment, it made no sense to me.

"How's your health, Auntie Coco?" I asked, trying to change the subject, to help Shak out.

"Oh, sama sama." She sighed. "My cholesterol's a bit high-lah, so the doctor wants me to go on a diet. Aiya, I told him, how am I going to go on a diet at my age?" Auntie Coco shook her head, and when she looked at Shak, her eyes were full of concern, but I thought it was only because of Shak's pregnancy. "You are healthy?"

Shak smiled. "Yes."

"We should be going now," I started to say, but Auntie Coco was already calling to her sister, "Babi, Babi, come out here for a while."

The sister smiled, but didn't rise from the chair. She went on holding the basket of peas, smiling as if she didn't have a care in the world, as they say.

"Auntie Coco," I started again.

She swatted at my words like mosquitoes, and stepped closer to Shak, who stepped closer to me at once, which surprised both me and Auntie Coco, although for different reasons. And it made Auntie Coco say, "Eh?" and look at Shak as if suddenly she was realizing, clairvoyant or not, she didn't really know Shak. Like everyone else, she had been making assumptions about her.

"I'm not going to eat you, girl," said Auntie Coco. "Why you scared of me like that?"

"Oh, I didn't mean that." Shak shook her head and gave Auntie Coco an embarrassed smile. "I'm sorry." Then she looked at me, but I didn't know what to say.

"Come, let me touch your baby."

Before we knew it, Auntie Coco had laid her hands on Shak's womb, and I saw her sister putting down the basket and getting up.

"Three months more. Make sure this Dr. Tay is a good doctor, okay? If you don't like him, come and see me. I give you someone."

That was what she said, Auntie Coco, although Shak was only five months pregnant.

"The baby's not due until the end of December, Auntie Coco," I said, since Shak wasn't saying anything.

"Three months," she repeated, removing her hands quite solemnly. She looked at Shak. "You listen to me, okay, girl? You get ready-ah."

Shak nodded and smiled. She didn't completely believe what Auntie Coco was saying, I could tell. I wondered whether to let her know about Auntie Coco and how she may have been born with a veil, but then I looked at that watermelon womb and thought, maybe it was better not to. In case the rumor about the baby ghost was indeed a rumor only, I didn't want to help Chandra to pantang Shak. Definitely, I didn't want to pantang her baby, such a helpless innocent.

Auntie Coco's sister had come out to the gate by now, and was standing and staring at Shak's womb. She was wearing one of her prettier dresses that evening, a floral print, I remember. Blue and yellow splashes of Danish tulips on a white background, very bright and free, as if she were going out somewhere, as if she were meeting up with a hot date, as they say. I wouldn't want to own a dress like that now, since you never know what can bring you bad luck, but it was certainly pretty.

"Howdee," said the sister, meaning "Howdy," of course, like a cowboy, only she couldn't speak that fast.

Shak smiled at her and said, "Hi, how are you?" very kindly, which maybe was what made the sister decide it was safe to come out to the road.

"She watch too much TV," said Auntie Coco, as her sister was opening the gate.

"You want some peas?" the sister asked, looking only at Shak and ignoring me completely. She could be like that sometimes.

"No, thank you." A few strands of hair fell over Shak's face as she shook her head, so gracefully, even in the heat. I saw both

Auntie Coco and the sister noticing it, as if only now were they seeing the auburn hue of Shak's hair, not black like the rest of ours. But who could miss seeing her hair the first time they saw her? It used to drive the boys wild, that hair, all the boys, Chinese, Malay, Indian, European, their background didn't matter when it came to Shak. Because of her hair, and also what some of the lay teachers used to call, Shak's six-million-dollar eyelashes (the teachers were punning, of course, on the six-million-dollar man, Lee Majors, the American actor).

"Babi," said Auntie Coco. "See?" And she put her hands on Shak's womb again, moving them around this time, a bit gingerly, as if to make sure not to disturb the baby while she measured the length and width of its head. That was how it looked to me, what Auntie Coco was doing, although maybe she was measuring something else, somehow.

The sister also put her hands on Shak's womb, and I looked at Shak to see if all this touching was making her uncomfortable. But Shak seemed quite at ease with it, you know. She was looking down, watching their hands, with her head tilted sideways, her beautiful hair falling against her cheek.

Other neighbors may have seen us out there, although there was still no one else outside, and Evelina Thumboo had gone back into her house.

I remember looking over at the jacaranda, its violet flowers spreading so delicately in the evening light. Evelina Thumboo's lamp was on, the usual one by her living-room window. Her curtains were open, I remember, and so were the curtains in most of our other neighbors' houses.

"Babi, what do you say?" Auntie Coco was asking.

"Boy," her sister replied, with a giggle. "Boy baby."

Auntie Coco smiled, looking pleased, and for some reason, I noticed the wrinkles around her eyes, as if she might be older than I used to think she was.

"You want a boy?" she asked Shak.

I already knew Shak's answer, although we hadn't talked much about her baby, you know.

"I want my baby," she told Auntie Coco. "Boy or girl, I don't care. I want my child." And there was something about the way she was looking at Auntie Coco, I remember it now. I saw it even then, but I couldn't place my finger on what was so odd about her expression, only that maybe, she was starting to believe Auntie Coco a bit.

"You have a boy. Ambitious also."

"How do you know?" I interrupted them, feeling a bit left out.

"Always kicking, right or not?" Auntie Coco went on, still talking to Shak.

"That's why you think it's a boy?" I asked, just to see what she would say. "Girl babies don't kick?"

Auntie Coco turned to me and asked, "You want to learn?" but her tone implied she knew I wouldn't go for it. "You want to learn, I can teach you."

I looked at Shak, who was watching me as if she were holding her tongue about something. But about what, I wasn't sure.

"We have to go," she said suddenly, to Auntie Coco and her sister. "My mum, you know. She doesn't like it when people are late for dinner."

"Ah, okay-lah," said Auntie Coco. "We talk some more another time. Go, better go-ah."

"Go," echoed the sister, and she reached out and patted Shak's womb as if for one last time.

And that was how we left them.

I THOUGHT SHAK would want to start talking right away about Auntie Coco. I thought she was going to ask me right away, whether or not I believed what Auntie Coco had foretold, but as it turned out, Shak didn't speak until we were almost at her house, and then, what she asked me was, "Do you know how Laura Timmerman's doing?"

Shak knew I wasn't in touch with most of our classmates, but I hadn't told her it was by intent. Because then I would have to tell her why, which would only drag up the fifteen years and how much I had missed her, and she hadn't found time even for a postcard. What would be the point, right? Better to move on with life, as they say.

So I lied a bit, although I felt uncomfortable doing it, since Shak and I weren't the sort to lie to each other. "She's fine," I said, and fortunately I had seen Laura's two children from afar once, when they were visiting their grandfather. So I was able to refer to them, only not by name. I told Shak, "She has two daughters. They're happy living in Australia."

"That's good," she murmured, and I wasn't sure which part she was remembering, but I thought, since she had asked about Laura Timmerman, perhaps her mind had drifted past that night to the following morning. To our school tuckshop where Laura Timmerman had told us (while Isabella was also there), how the doctor and his wife had made their son strip off his pajamas in the driveway, first the shirt, then the trousers, right where all the neighbors could see, as well as anyone passing by the house, man or woman, boy or girl.

All Laura's neighbors could do was stay away from their windows. Keep their own faces out of sight. Laura and her cousin who was visiting, they had heard everything from upstairs in Laura's bedroom, how the son kept begging and begging, "Please-lah Daddy, please don't make me do it," when his father was telling him to take off his trousers.

By the time Shak and I were stepping off the bus, he was already fully naked, the son, and whimpering as he was being dragged towards the gate. Thirteen years old, I remember, younger than us. A St. Peter's boy. His hips so pale in the amber light, his penis sticking out like a carrot every time the doctor grabbed his arm to prevent him from covering himself.

"How could a father do that to his own child?" Shak was saying, as if she were reading my mind. It was the same thing she had said on the night itself, when finally, we were able to make ourselves walk away.

"I don't know," I said, just as I had said before. Had Shak been thinking about the doctor's son, the whole time Auntie Coco and her sister had been touching her womb, and making predictions about her baby? I wondered about it, but I couldn't make myself ask the question. Not that I had forgotten anything, certainly not what Shak and I had grown up hearing about the boy's sister, how she had been kidnapped when she was four, and molested and then murdered. (Her body wasn't found for two weeks, another of our unsolved cases. Maybe that was why, because there was no one else to blame, the parents kept punishing the son.) But I knew how to put things on the back burner, so to speak. Because I didn't want to become obsessed with the past. I wanted to move on, not be like Americans, everyone going into therapy.

But the other side to the story was that at fifteen, Shak wasn't meeting boys in the cemetery, yet. Neither of us had ever seen a naked boy, you know. We hadn't even seen naked girls, because in school, for P.E. everyone would change into shorts and T-shirts in the bathroom stalls, all of us protecting our modesty in those days.

So being Americanized, maybe that was why, even after we had seen the doctor's house, Shak couldn't put it behind her easily.

That was what I told myself, because I didn't want to think she might be holding on to it on purpose. Because I wanted to move on, as I've said.

So I brought us back to Auntie Coco.

"What do you think about what Auntie Coco said?" I asked Shak. "You think the baby might be born early?"

"Maybe," she said. "But the baby's not a boy."

"You've already found out?"

"No. I just have a feeling."

We were passing Willy Coleman's house, I remember, his front door closed, curtains drawn across all the windows downstairs as usual. (Because he was a very private man, that Willy Coleman, and his wife, being from China, she had never tried to have much say about anything, and their son was only eleven years old. He had even less say, that poor Matthew. Always getting caned for one thing or another, you know.)

Next door to Willy Coleman's house was his mother's house, and I could see Adelaide Coleman's other grandson, the older one who lived with her, Nathan, talking on the telephone in the living room. He was standing near a window, smiling and laughing and shrugging his shoulders this way and that. Probably talking to a girl, and no wonder. Because he was becoming quite a heart-throb, that boy. Like Ivan Anthony in our time, I could see it coming already, and I wondered vaguely whether Adelaide would be able to control him, or was it true that every child needed at least two parents?

Shak hadn't told me anything about the baby's father, but I was sure she would tell me eventually. Maybe she could sense I didn't want to talk about it, yet, which I myself wasn't aware of. Only looking back now, I see it may have been what was going on with me.

"Do you think she's right?" Shak asked me, as we reached her gate.

I was surprised, because I thought for sure, she would remember why Auntie Coco might call the baby a boy if the baby was actually a girl. To deceive the spirits, of course, to confuse them in case they came looking for a newborn. Which sometimes, spirits would do, come looking for a newborn, for whatever reason.

So I told her, "Yes, Auntie Coco's right. She's one of those women, okay? She can tell about things like that."

Shak looked at me for a moment, and I could feel her uncertainty over what to say, as if again, she was holding something back. Then she asked, "Are you sure about her? This Auntie Coco. She's reliable?"

And I was relieved. Because we shouldn't have been talking so openly about it, you know, especially standing on the road like that.

Not that the cemetery, which was only several feet away, the air there dusky with the approaching night, with the aroma of frangipani and jasmine damp like dew on the leaves, not that it was anything to fear, or Che' Halimah even. But who could tell who or what might be listening?

Whether the baby ghost was more than a rumor, or not.

"Yes," I told Shak. "Auntie Coco's reliable."

And it seemed to be all she needed to hear.

MOST OF THE neighbors were home that evening, Evelina Thumboo, as I've already said, and Gopal Dharma, his car was parked in the driveway when we had passed by his house. Also, the baskets left by the two girls were gone by then. (We hadn't seen the girls that afternoon, but their baskets had been there when Shak and I had passed the house earlier. Jo and Susanna, who would come every Friday to weed Gopal Dharma's garden. We had seen their baskets on the front step, so they must have left by the time we were leaving for our walk.) My mother wasn't home, since she was at Holy Family, playing gin rummy with Father O'Hara and Sister Sylvia. Because that was her act of charity, as my mother would say, and every Friday evening, it was where she went, to Holy Family, and she would stay there sometimes as late as ten o'clock. Willy Coleman was home, and Adelaide, too, and Wong Siew Chin and her husband Jeremy, and Serena and Ivan. All of them would come outside later, I remember, when Auntie Coco started calling for her sister.

Sally Soo-Tho would come out as well, and Bernadette Tan, who was good friends with my mother (even though my mother was always complaining about her). Wong Siew Chin was also friends with my mother, but she was closer friends with Dorothy Neo (who I don't think was home). Those were the yakkity-yaks, the main ones. Sally Soo-Tho and Bernadette Tan couldn't have seen Shak and me when we were outside Auntie Coco's house, because their houses were too far up the slope. But they were only a few doors away from Shak's house, you know. They may have seen us outside Shak's gate, since we were there talking for a while.

Later, when people were going over the night, no one would say anything about a baby ghost, or about any girl hovering nearby. As if none of our neighbors could see her, not one of them, not even Auntie Coco.

So where had that rumor begun?

Shak was standing beside me, waiting, as I closed the gate after us. We could smell her mother's mutton curry, rich and spicy, coming from the back of the house, and I was thinking, at that moment, about Isabella. I was thinking of Isabella coming to the library that afternoon, and on the morning Laura Timmerman was telling everyone about the doctor's son (how after the doctor had pushed him outside the gate, he had crawled underneath a neighbor's car parked on the road, and he had hidden there until a servant was sent to get him, when it was almost midnight). I was thinking about Isabella watching Shak, the whole time Laura was talking, and when Shak finally noticed, the two of them had exchanged looks, just for a quick second, and then they had turned away from each other.

Since Shak had never spoken to me about it, I must have thought after a while, I had imagined it. But I hadn't, you know.

"Rose?"

I knew from her tone, Shak was thinking I wanted to say something, but there wasn't anything to say. So I shook my head, and I answered, "Nothing."

"You sure?"

Her American accent sounded stronger when I couldn't see her face clearly, since by now, the sun had gone down. That's how I remember the moment, not because it bothered me to hear the accent. Because on that other night, we were standing like that also, although it was later in the night, and she had asked my name like a question. Only then, her voice was still Singaporean, and young, so young. I wasn't sure when I had felt her lips touching mine what was happening, whether she was kissing me or not, and I've never been sure.

It was only that one time.

"Rose."

"There's nothing, Shak. Really." I shook my head again, and I thought I heard her sigh, but then, she said quietly, "Okay."

And we left the gate and went into the house, and we weren't outside again until Auntie Coco came up the road, which was shortly after eight o'clock.

OCCURRENCES ON THE
THIRD SUNDAY
IN

august, 1994

LULU MENDEZ

U NLIKE THE WINDOWS in Madam's living room and most of
the windows around the house, the ones in Madam's bedroom had never been replaced (as Madam's husband had fallen ill
while the other windows were being replaced and with the workers
hammering and drilling and walking in and out of the house all day,
it had been impossible for anyone in the family to find a moment's
calm, and so Madam had decided to pay the contractor before the
job was finished, saying she would get in touch with him when her
husband was better, which Malika was sure Madam had intended to
do and would have, if things hadn't started going downhill so quickly, it seemed there had barely been time to catch one's breath).

So the windows in Madam's bedroom were the original windows of the house, with frosted panes and rusted levers and latches that in recent years had come unlocked on their own on a few blustery afternoons. Malika had never known the latches to loosen on a still night, so when Madam mentioned while she was sipping from her cup of coffee on Sunday morning that the window near the dressing table had been ajar when she woke up, Malika wondered at first if it was possible that she, Malika, had forgotten to lock it on the night before. (On the night before, Malika had heated up some left-over fish curry and eaten it with freshly cooked rice while she read by herself at the kitchen table. Madam had been out having dinner with a recently widowed friend, an American gentleman named Nigel, who used to be a friend of Madam's husband's. She had come home around ten o'clock, while Malika was still awake, but Malika hadn't known she would, and at half-past nine when Malika was closing the windows, she had gone into Madam's room to close those windows as well, which she would have left open if she had known Madam was on her way home, as Madam often liked to listen to the rhythms of the night (as Madam put it) before she went to sleep. Malika would find her sitting on her bed and looking towards the windows after reading or writing a letter (a page or a pen still in Madam's hand) when she brought her the usual glass of whiskey. There would be such an expression in Madam's eyes, Malika would say each time she stumbled upon this moment in her story. Such an expression, whether of yearning or relief, Malika was hard put to define as she shook her head and sighed, her fingers reaching for her red bead, for its resplendent smoothness and its absolute fit between her thumb and finger. Madam had never admitted it to her, but it wasn't lost on Malika that it was Madam's husband who hadn't been able to tolerate any length of a time in a room without an air conditioner, at least not in Singapore. Ever since his death, she was no longer required to turn on the air conditioner in the master bedroom a half hour before Madam was expected home.)

"I suppose it's high time we replace them-lah," Madam was saying, and when Malika looked back upon the morning, it always began this way, with Madam sitting at the kitchen table in her green-and-yellow floral pajamas (a hint of fuchsia lipstick from the night before still on Madam's lips), Madam's long, slim fingers folded around the steaming white cup as if to warm her hands. Malika would remember the sensation of being as if in a book, as if in a scene set in a foreign country on one of those brisk winter mornings imbued with a slant of light (or was it supposed to be on winter afternoons that the foreign poet had seen the slant of light?), as if Madam were a character she was encountering in some such place, a woman alone at breakfast in a house inundated with absences. (One could almost hear the timber crackling in a stone hearth to her left, just out of Malika's angle of vision, and a dry wind rasping behind her head, as if outside the kitchen window were bare, wiry trees and the sky ablaze in a chilling temperate light.)

"Would you like more toast, Madam?" she asked, even though Madam hadn't yet touched the two slices Malika had left on a plate on the table when she had brought Madam her coffee and *The Sunday Times* (which was lying unread beside the plate, the corners of the newsprint pages still flat and uncrinkled).

"No, Malika, thank you," was Madam's response, and Malika could hear in Madam's tone that Madam was preoccupied with a matter other than breakfast.

She herself had spoken only to break the delirium of feeling afloat on a page, as if she, too, were a character, wandering on the outskirts of the house owned by the woman at the table, the woman who tended to occupy the heart of any book, who dined alone now, on most days and nights, but who had once been married and surrounded by daughters (before they were teenagers and started spending more and more hours out of the house) and who used to dine every so often with the numerous friends and colleagues of her husband's, the woman who sometimes went out with a friend of her own, the wife of a colleague of her husband's or another schoolteacher (or sometimes one of Madam's cousins would visit from Malacca), and very, very occasionally, now that the woman's husband was deceased, went out on what might be called a date.

Unless they were about war and even when they were set in wartime, stories tended to revolve around dates, every story a romance of some sort, Malika thought as she stepped into the passageway outside the kitchen to gather pieces of hand-washed laundry from the clothesline (there were two of Madam's sleeveless silk-knit tops, one in solid apple-green, the other an effervescent blue, and a dazzling mauve sari Madam had worn to a farewell luncheon for one of the nuns at school on Thursday, a young nun who, like Miss Shakilah, had been one of Madam's pupils and who would be leaving in a few days to study in the master's program in psychology at the University of Chicago in America).

It crossed Malika's mind (as it had on other occasions) that she had never experienced a date but she simply reminded herself (as she would on other occasions) that dating was a modern invention, a modern luxury and, in some respects, a frivolous pastime (to be enjoyed by the very young or by a widow like Madam who wasn't seeking another marriage). Romance wasn't a necessary human experience and the lack of it wasn't an issue worth dwelling upon (Malika's exact words, from what I remember). Having acquiesced before she was Sali's age or mine to her apparent lack of sex appeal in the eyes of men, and to the compounding unattractiveness of her station in life, Malika's indulgence of Sali's daydreams bore no reflection on her wishes for herself. No boys had ever whistled at her when she was a schoolgirl at the convent in Malacca, and not even the roguish-looking, blue-collar characters slouching over the tables at Newton paid her any mind when she accompanied

Madam. It was no wonder then that she believed and acted on the conviction that romance lay beyond her realm of possibilities, for Malika knew no gentleman was going to come calling for her at Madam's gate, or try to steal a kiss from her at the end of the night, or send her roses in the middle of an ordinary day.)

"Eh, Malika, can you go to Holland Village this morning and buy some steaks?" asked Madam.

Malika lay her hand on the apple-green top, feeling the expensive Chinese silk like a caress on the calloused skin of her palm. She paused to say, "Yes, Madam, how many?"

"Just two will do," said Madam. "Two thick and juicy T-bones, or three if you feel like having one today, you want one?"

"No, thank you, Madam." (Malika wasn't religious but she had never acquired a liking for beef, which she had tasted once as a young girl, at Madam's request.) "Mrs. Allen coming for lunch today, Madam?" she asked, folding the apple-green top and laying it on a clean corner of the dryer.

"No-lah, I can't meet with her today, although poor thing, I think she gets lonely without her husband. Miss Shakilah is coming over."

"Oh, I see, Madam."

"Let's also have baked potatoes and buttered peas, with sour cream on the side, just as they do it at the American Club. Okay, Malika?"

"Yes, Madam."

Reaching for the blue top, Malika noticed out of the corner of her eye the burst of sunlight in the flamboyant trees, rampant streams of gold over the branches and leaves, the crimson flowers edged in shadow sparkling and provocative on this morning. Her armpits felt damp with perspiration. She wondered as she was folding the blue top if she would dare to ask Miss Shakilah how Miss Shakilah had known about the girl in the sugar cane, and why she had asked Malika about it.

"So remember to buy sour cream-ah, when you go to the

supermarket? And check to see if we need a new bottle of Worcestershire sauce before you go. Jangan lupa, okay?"

"No, I won't forget, Madam." Malika decided that if the opportunity arose, she would ask Miss Shakilah why she had asked about the girl, but only if the opportunity arose (which it would not).

A mournful howl rose from one of the neighboring gardens as she lay the blue top on top of the apple-green (a howl unlike that of any dog or cat, Malika would muse later when the memory returned swollen with other, wilder sounds, later when uncertainty flowered gasping and sputtering into a conundrum of meaning and the seething echo of things buried in monsoon mud lay imprinted on the wall of her womb, not like an embryo but like the thought of an embryo, Malika would say).

For the moment it seemed a Sunday like any other. Only the mynah birds were oddly subdued, their presence a limp fluttering somewhere in the air or a feathery brush through the grass. But Malika was sure she sensed the sharp note of a warble beginning in the treetops as she reached for Madam's sari, careful to fold it in layers as she lifted it off the clothesline so that the ends didn't even skim the ground.

She wouldn't remember hearing Madam getting up from the table and leaving the room, but when Malika turned towards the doorway, Madam was no longer in the kitchen. She thought nothing of it, however, when she saw that the plate of toast was empty and *The Sunday Times* wasn't on the table. (Madam had probably taken the paper into the bathroom to read, as was Madam's habit.)

A ball rolled out of the neighbor's house next-door and Malika heard it bouncing along the stone slabs that covered the neighbor's drain. No child ran out to pick it up, and when Malika glanced towards the fence before stepping into the kitchen, she saw the ball rolling onto the grass and coming to rest by a banana tree.

This, she would remember.

● ● ●

WHAT MALIKA DIDN'T know about Miss Shakilah wasn't important or relevant to the turn her life was about to take (and remains
hearsay in our story, which is to say, one wouldn't hear about this
in the daily, chatty conversations of the Madams in Miss Shakilah's neighborhood, but only in the most private of conversations muttered among the servants, and this is simply that in
reality, Miss Shakilah wasn't the paragon of virtue Madam and
Malika had believed her to be in school, for while it was true Miss
Shakilah had been a straight A's pupil, in the months before her
departure for America in 1979 she was rumored to have been the
more ardent pursuer of a forbidden affair between her and one of
her neighbors, one of Miss Shakilah's female neighbors, a certain
lovely and reclusive Madam Thumboo, a widow, who was not
only a woman but also old enough to have given birth to Miss
Shakilah herself, who was, indeed, exactly the same age as Miss
Shakilah's mother, and Miss Shakilah herself being only eighteen
at the time of the affair . . . where did she find the nerve? a few of
us had wanted to know and it's this that lingers on our minds).

It was just as well Malika didn't know (and fortuitous that
Madam lived in Bukit Timah, a great distance away from us), as
Malika might not have agreed so easily to the proposal about to
be put forth by Madam Thumboo in a few months when Miss
Shakilah went into labor (and if Malika hadn't said yes to
Madam Thumboo, there's no telling what would have been
done about the baby).

Of course the hint of what would come to pass was in the
air when Miss Shakilah arrived for lunch on the Sunday following Madam Coco's sister's vanishing, but it was the merest hint.

Malika was removing Madam's set of bamboo placemats
from the top drawer of the rosewood sideboard in the dining
room when she heard Madam greeting Miss Shakilah in the
front of the house . . .

"Hello, darling, how are you feeling today?"

Malika heard Miss Shakilah's soft laugh and a low murmur as Miss Shakilah was taking off her sandals on the patio. (When she brought Miss Shakilah a glass of soya bean milk, she saw the sandals positioned neatly to the side of the doormat, clumsy-looking brown Birkenstocks that reminded Malika of a water buffalo's hoofs. Malika had seen such footwear on the feet of the European tourists, too, and sometimes on the feet of local teenagers loitering about on Orchard Road, where Malika used to accompany Madam so that she could run errands for Madam while Madam was at the beauty salon—this happened infrequently now as Madam liked running her own errands, liked the feel of competence and self-sufficiency that came in the small act of taking care of oneself.)

Nothing seemed awry, as Malika would tell us months later, after Madam Thumboo had been to see her and when we heard of Madam's seemingly sudden decision to put the house up for sale. (Needless to say, Sali and I were dismayed at the news, but we're not the point of this story. We've been only eavesdroppers here, peering over Malika's shoulder while she rummages through her years with Madam, her fingers turning over leaves of glances and speechless moments for the lost unspoken, the missed unsaid but understood thread of their conversations that could have foretold their story's end.)

It was around noon or a little past it that Madam and Miss Shakilah sat down to lunch (in the dining room rather than in the kitchen, where Malika had laid the table with a white lace tablecloth crocheted by Madam's mother, utensils made of English silver, and Madam's expensive white chinaware and crystal stemware—Madam herself had arranged the tall cattleya orchids Miss Shakilah had brought in a crystal vase and set them in the center of the table, varying hues of pink and brilliant amber opening off the bifoliate bulbs and imparting to the table an elegantly festive touch).

The sliding doors to the garden were open and a mynah bird was skipping along the top of the British neighbor's wall. Malika drew the sheer gauze curtains together, to keep out the sun's glare as the afternoon wore on. She thought she sensed Miss Shakilah's gaze following her around the table as she walked towards the standing fan in the corner by the piano, but Malika could have been mistaken about it as when she turned around (after switching on the fan and setting it to rotate at medium speed), Miss Shakilah was shaking her head and smiling at Madam (who was giving Miss Shakilah an account of her dinner date with Nigel), and looking at Madam with such muted adoration and affection, Malika wondered how she could have forgotten that expression of Miss Shakilah's from when Miss Shakilah had been a pupil of Madam's, for now the picture came flashing back of a sad-faced schoolgirl with plaited hair, sitting among her classmates on the patio floor and singing her bruised heart to ashes.

(It was this memory of Miss Shakilah at twelve that would prompt Malika to say yes to Madam Thumboo's proposal, but the event had yet to happen and as Malika was leaving the dining room, she felt merely grateful that life had never shown her such an expression on Michelle's face, or Caroline's or Francesca's.)

"And then, when we were sitting in his living room, he kept putting his hand on my lap, you know?" Madam was saying as Malika stepped into the corridor.

She paused to listen through the wall.

"You were surprised?" asked Miss Shakilah, with a smile in her voice.

"Of course I was surprised. Alamak, you, as bad as my daughters-lah, you. You know what Caroline said when I told her? Mum, ask him if he has a slow touch. Can you believe it? I told her see-lah, here I was feeling sorry for the poor man because his wife just died, and I look down and there's his hand on my lap.

I didn't know what to do with his hand, I told her. Ask him if he has a slow touch. That's what she said, my Caroline."

In the back of the house, a sudden gust shook the banyan trees, and Malika could hear the quiet moan of the bending leaves as Madam and Miss Shakilah went on talking. She closed her eyes (because there seemed to be whispers lapping about the corridor on this afternoon and as Malika would put it later, somewhere in the recesses of her mind she could feel a flickering, a hearkening of sorts towards a forgotten life, the one not lived, as Madam's and Miss Shakilah's voices receded momentarily). She was on the verge of hearing something else (Malika was sure of this) when one of Madam's bedroom windows came unhinged and started banging against the sill.

Malika opened her eyes. As she made her way towards the bedroom, Madam was asking Miss Shakilah what Miss Shakilah had decided to do about her book, if Miss Shakilah had received enlightenment yet.

She heard Miss Shakilah laugh as another gust swept across Madam's garden, and the window in the bedroom banged again on the sill.

S O WE WERE at the parish house on Sunday afternoon, two weeks after the Friday that Auntie Coco's sister went missing. Ya-lah, this time, Dorothy, Siew Chin, Bernadette and I were all present, but they're useless-lah, the others. No use asking them to tell about that Sunday. Probably, they'll say they can't remember. So frightened they were when they saw the old lady, and Dorothy and Siew Chin didn't even know about the other incidents. Imagine if they did. (I'm sure Dorothy would have found out from her Lulu if the girl had been home that Saturday, although now as I'm thinking about it, Lulu could have heard about it from other people's servants also. No-lah, I don't know who's friends with whom in those circles, but I think Lulu used to be friends with Teresa Albuquerque's girl. Anyway, it was quite a shock to Dorothy, you know, when her Lulu won that writing contest. Ya-lah, I also was surprised, but it's just as well, bukan? Why pay money for a servant who only wants to read books? Right or not? But anyway, we ourselves had ended up not telling Dorothy or Siew Chin about that Saturday, Bernadette because she was already scared stiff, in spite of her usual skepticism, and I was trying to sort things out without anyone's interference, for a change.)

Ya-lah, there's someone else you could ask, but she's living overseas now, and I don't think she's ever coming back.

In my opinion, the day had already started out strangely, because first of all, what was Ying Ying Coleman doing by herself in the market that morning? And why, of all people, did she choose Siew Chin to talk to? Especially about such personal matters. Right or not? Ya, ya, I know what Siew Chin thought, that it was because Willy Coleman was sick and someone had to do the shopping. But they could have sent the son, Matthew. He was old enough by now. My point is this. That Willy Coleman would never have let his precious wife out of his sight just like that. Three hundred dollars, that's how much I hear he paid for her, plus airfare of course. She had advertised her face in a Hong Kong brochure-lah, and somehow or other, the brochure had fallen into Willy's lap. Men with money can get whatever they want, bukan? See how hard it is to find true love.

"Not just like that," Siew Chin insisted when I pointed out how Willy had never before, not even once, allowed Ying Ying out of the house without him by her side, or rather, in front of her. "He's sick-lah, I told you."

As if the fellow had never been sick before. Come hell or high water, Ying Ying had never disobeyed her husband, okay? And no wonder-lah, if what Ying Ying had told Siew Chin was the truth. *Wah, the names he shouts at her when they're making love.*

Bastard-lah. Bloody bitch-lah. And then, according to Siew Chin, Ying Ying had asked whether Jeremy called her the same names or different names when they were making love. Imagine. How unlucky some women can be, ya? That Ying Ying had no idea what marriage was all about. To have and to hold, to love and to cherish. That's what marriage is supposed to be. Thank heavens my Hock Siew and I always had true love between us, even if we weren't rich. You see how money isn't everything.

Of course, Dorothy was backing Siew Chin up, and Bernadette wasn't saying anything, sitting there buat-bodoh-lah, pretending only, as if she wasn't interested. She tried to look as if she wasn't even listening, as if she was just enjoying the breeze from the window, and hearing only the rustling of the angsana leaves. (By now, the tree's been chopped down, but in those days, it was there outside the window, one lovely old angsana. Such a stupid thing, to chop it down.)

"He's probably never been this sick," Dorothy said. "Must be pneumonia or something like that. He probably can't even get out of bed."

"Ah, ya, that's what Ying Ying said." Siew Chin nodded her head, as if she had just remembered this part. "He's been bedridden for a few days already."

"Has he seen a doctor?" I asked, because if it was that serious, a doctor would have been called to the house, right? And someone would have noticed, even if not one of us.

Siew Chin shrugged her shoulders. "Don't know-lah, I didn't want to pry. But he must have, ya?" She looked at Dorothy. "I think you're right. Must be pneumonia. One of Jeremy's friends at the office also has it."

Listen to her, as if an epidemic was just around the corner. She and Dorothy were never that good at weeding out the truth. Always jumping too easily to conclusions, the two of them.

Everything's connected-lah. It must be, bukan?

. . .

OKAY, SO I was the one who had volunteered the four of us to make the wayang puppets. (That was why we were at Holy Family that afternoon, in the parish house dining room where the huge teak table was.) And no, I wasn't trying to gain favor with Father Pereira, as some of the other ladies wanted to think. I don't mean Dorothy or Siew Chin or Bernadette. I mean the other church ladies—that Juniper Ang, for instance, who had been jealous of my pineapple tarts for years. I suppose she fancied herself quite the pastry chef-lah, must be. And Teresa Albuquerque. She also was jealous, but not over the pineapple tarts. She had been wanting to join our clique, just so she could boast to us at close range about her children, and how well they were doing. Compared to my Rose-lah, that was what she meant each time she managed to catch me off guard. Who was she kidding? As if I was a dummy and didn't know how to read between the lines. So now she was getting her revenge, helping to spread rumors about how I wanted to be another Megan Thornbird. None of it was true. She and the other ladies were the ones with crushes on Father Pereira, but you see how they were. Too lazy to volunteer for the puppets, and then complaining about it.

Father Pereira himself had approached us, not the other way around. You should have seen Dorothy's and Siew Chin's faces when I said okay. Bernadette, she was going along with anything I decided now, which should have made Dorothy and Siew Chin sit up and take notice, but it didn't, for some funny reason.

Of course the teenagers had gone to Father Pereira instead of Father O'Hara, not only because he was the chief parish priest. They knew Father O'Hara, ya? Definitely, the old chap would have put his foot down, but once they got Father Pereira to say yes, what could Father O'Hara do? Especially given his announcement a few years ago that he was going to step back and let Father Pereira take charge, as if Father Pereira wasn't already in charge. It was just that Father O'Hara had been around longer-lah, so Father Pereira would often let him have his way. Actually, they didn't get along, you know. Father O'Hara had been quite disappointed when Father Pereira had first joined us, because Father Pereira turned out to be so different from his predecessor, Father D'Souza, who, if you can believe this, got sent to Africa after being with us for thirteen years. Imagine. That's what the Vatican does-lah, to make sure priests don't get attached to places, since they're to be in the world but not of it. Only Father O'Hara, for some reason, ended up staying with us for practically his whole life. Why he was never made chief parish priest, I don't know. Could be due to a lack of education, since Father D'Souza and Father Pereira had both attended universities (in Rome, no less), and had all kinds of degrees, although in my opinion, it isn't necessary for a priest to have an advanced degree. But you know the Vatican. No use trying to argue with the Pope or the bishops.

Ah, so anyway, we got Father Pereira and right from the start, the teenagers loved him. No wonder, bukan? Let me tell you what Belinda Wong found in his car when she borrowed it one day to visit the hospitals. One whole bunch of rock-and-roll cassettes, they were strewn all over the passenger seat. Elvis Presley-lah, B. B. King-lah, Chuck Berry, the Temptations, the Supremes, et cetera. *You name it, Father Pereira has it*, Belinda said.

It's obvious-lah, what he must have thought when the teenagers asked him if they could put up a wayang kulit. *Wah*, he must have thought, *it's good that they want to do something with cultural value.* Of course Father O'Hara would have objected on the grounds of paganism, but if you ask me, he could be a bit too conservative-lah. Must live and let live, bukan?

But luckily, both of them were out that afternoon. You know how priests tend to disapprove of rumors. If I remember correctly, Father Pereira was doing some house blessings in the neighborhood, and Father O'Hara as usual was giving Communion at the old folks' home. Sister Sylvia was not around, either. She always went over to the convent on Sundays, to do what, I don't know, but actually, it wouldn't have mattered even if she had been around. That nun's so pekak. As deaf as a doornail. (That was another reason our poker games always lasted so long. Everything you said to her, you had to say at least three, four times.)

So anyway, there we were. We were at the embroidering stage—only after all the puppets' clothes were embroidered, then we were going to sew the parts of the bodies together. You should always sew the parts together last, ya? To make sure everything fits. Of course our puppets were not as elaborate as the traditional kind-lah, since ours were made out of cardboard. This was for charity, what, so never mind-lah. That was what Father Pereira had assured us, and I was quite relieved, to tell you the truth. Who knows how many mistakes we would have made if we had tried to use wood or leather. Sometimes perfectionism can be a downfall. So ya-lah, luckily, Father Pereira must have considered the fact that none of us were experts.

You know the dining room at Holy Family, full of crucifixes on the walls. Bernadette also was glad to have an excuse to spend her afternoons there, okay? That was why-lah she had kept her mouth shut when I had volunteered us. (You see how when she didn't want to be a coconut-head, she didn't have to be.)

You understand what I'm saying? Remember, Shakilah hadn't given birth, yet. Don't forget what I've said about Pontianak and the Langsuir.

So anyway, Siew Chin and Dorothy were still going on about that Ying Ying.

"How did she talk about it?" Dorothy wanted to know. "Did her voice show any emotion or not?"

"Ya-lah, but a bit only," Siew Chin said.

"Some women, it turns them on, you know." That was Bernadette, deciding to join in after she had been buat-bodohing long enough.

"Turns them on?" Siew Chin shook her head, with great indignation, I might add. "You mean, you think women can get aroused by that sort of treatment? You gila?"

"Different strokes for different folks," Bernadette told her. "What, don't tell me you've never heard the saying."

"Please-lah, don't test my patience."

You see how I wasn't the only one who ever got irritated by Bernadette and her way of talking. Didn't I tell you? But Dorothy as always, trust her to save the day.

"Poor thing," she said. "Coming all this way to marry a man like that."

Ya-lah, she was right. Who would want to be in that boat, after all? Imagine your own husband calling you *Bitch, Bastard, Bitch, Bastard,* just as you're on the verge of bliss. How to enjoy making love like that? Plus, what about the son, ya? Imagine having to listen to your father behave that way. No wonder the boy doesn't come home nowadays, even with the father gone. Too many bad memories in the house, must be. If I were that Ying Ying, I would move to another house. There's no reason for her to stay.

But can't tell-lah what goes through people's heads some-times, especially one China-born-and-bred like her. Sometimes, it's all a mystery. And sometimes, truth is stranger than fiction.

YA. YA. ON the one hand, it may have been a coincidence. On the other hand, maybe not. As I've said, it was Father Pereira who had asked us if we would make the puppets. I didn't volunteer out of the blue, okay? Could be, the four of us were meant to be there that afternoon. Right or not? Otherwise, there wouldn't have been anyone to corroborate Alice Wang's daughter's story about the old lady calling to her to go behind the parish house. Even I wouldn't have known whether or not to believe a teenager. Ya, that girl Susanna (the one already fated to die in a boating accident when she was only seventeen, poor thing). You remember her mother Alice Wang, that pretty young widow who used to live up the road, next door to Regina Lim. Their two girls were best friends, okay, when they were growing up. Susanna was the quiet one-lah. She and Regina's daughter would remind me of Rose and Shakilah. Must be, when two friends end up being that close, one must always turn out quieter. Otherwise, how to tell them apart?

Of course, I've never had the experience-lah. You see who I had for a childhood friend. Bernadette. (Why is there the saying, birds of a feather flock together? See-lah, how conventional wisdom isn't always true.)

Ah, so anyway, as I was saying, Bernadette was already scared stiff from what had happened to the two of us. Ya-lah, she was covering it up quite well, but mark my words. She wasn't ready for yet one more thing, okay? Dorothy and Siew Chin also, they would rather wipe that afternoon out of their minds completely.

Here's what happened.

It was just after Dorothy noticed there was a finger missing from the puppet's hand. No-lah, I can't remember which puppet it was, but it didn't matter-lah.

"Alamak, you," I heard her say, so I looked up.

Here's how we were sitting—Dorothy was across from me, Siew Chin was to her right, and Bernadette was at the head of the table and closest to the window. I was on Bernadette's right, facing the hallway, with the window over my left shoulder and Father O'Hara's antique clock ticking on the wall behind my head. (You know which one I mean, with the rosewood body, still there hanging between the ivory crucifix and the Sacred Heart portrait of Our Lord. One of the parishioners had brought it back from abroad and given it to Father O'Hara, no one really knows why-lah. But must be, the parishioner had confessed something quite terrible and Father O'Hara had given him a lighter penance to do than he had deserved. That's my guess.)

So anyway, Siew Chin was the one who had cut out the puppets' limbs. We had put Bernadette in charge of the torsos, and Dorothy and I were doing the heads. So Dorothy was holding the arm in one hand and the puppet's sleeve in the other, as she looked at Siew Chin. (She must have been fitting the sleeve on top of the arm-lah, when she had noticed the missing finger.)

Siew Chin didn't notice anything at first, because she was looking at Dorothy's face, not at her hands. "What?" she asked.

"You see-lah your handiwork," Dorothy told her, but of course, her tone was affectionate. The two of them had been childhood friends, ya? Whether best friends or not, that, I never asked-lah. (No-lah, I didn't know them before we became neighbors. Before, they used to live in the Serangoon area. Quite lucky for them that they kept ending up living so close to each other. Of course, you see how everyone's luck evens out in the end. Now that Siew Chin's moved to Germany, I don't think they've continued to talk on the phone more than a few times a year.)

Siew Chin sighed when she saw the hand. "Aiya, you think they'll mind?" she asked.

Right at that moment, we heard the scream. It was soft and brief, not ear-piercing at all, but definitely it contained fear.

You remember I've said, I was facing the hallway. First of all, anyone entering the parish house, we would have heard, and the only way to reach the back was to walk down the hallway past us, okay? Nowadays, it's different because the garden fence is gone. (It was removed when the angsana tree got chopped down, to create an illusion of having more space, or something like that-lah.) But that Sunday, it was still there, enclosing Father O'Hara's rose bushes to protect them from vandalism, since this area was more rural back then, and various Toms, Dicks and Harrys were always passing by the church compound.

Ya, ya, believe it or not, there used to be rose bushes in the garden. Gorgeous blossoms, huge and red. Everyone wondered how they could survive the heat, but Father O'Hara had quite a green thumb-lah, must be. Some of the ladies tried to get the secret from him, but you've heard how he was. Always promising he would tell when he was on his deathbed, as if he could foresee the hour that would happen, which of course, he couldn't. So that's why now, those rose bushes have long been dug up. Ya-lah, they started dying the very next day after Father O'Hara passed away from a sudden heart attack.

So anyway, the old lady was squatting near one of the bushes, near the papaya tree (the one still there). And Susanna, poor girl, she was standing at the fence, not in the garden but on the other side, and you could see how she was shivering. Her face so puchat, we knew at once something was wrong. Of course, all of us had rushed out to the back to see who had screamed, and as soon as I saw the lady, I wondered how she had managed to walk past the dining room without my noticing, but at the time, I thought it was possible I had been looking away-lah. Maybe when she had walked past, I was concentrating on my embroidery. That was what I thought at first. As I've said, I don't jump to conclusions by force of habit, ya?

What else was strange was that Susanna was over at the fence by herself. Regina's daughter, that Jo, she was nowhere around, and as I've already pointed out, those two were always together, bukan? But I didn't think about this until later-lah, and neither did the others. Dorothy and Siew Chin, they were staring at the old lady as if trying to see if they could recognize her, as if one of the parishioners would be squatting in the garden like that. Betul-betul they also acted like coconut-heads sometimes. Bernadette, you can imagine-lah the panic building up in her, and to be honest, I wasn't feeling so calm myself.

At first, we couldn't see her face, the old lady. Her body was turned a bit to the right, in Susanna's direction, and she had a twig in her left hand which she was using to write or draw something on the ground. You know those patches of sand around the papaya tree where there's no grass. That's what the old lady was doing when we got to the back door. (That's where we had stopped short, after catching sight of Susanna and seeing the way she looked at us. Fear was written clearly in the poor girl's eyes, like a warning to us-lah, not to approach the lady.)

Definitely, she was holding the twig in her left hand. Until this day, I can't get rid of the image. That twig, bent slightly in the middle, moving here and there across the sand, and the lady's skirt draped over her knees. Ah, ya, she was wearing a full long skirt. Sky-blue, that's what the color is called now. That was the color of her skirt. And it was so long, it hid her feet.

Only when the lady lifted her head and turned to stare directly at the four of us, then we betul-betul terkejut, really startled.

All I can do is pray I never get that old. I pray Our Lord will show me mercy.

AH, SO HERE'S the hardest part to believe, but it's all true. Suddenly, as the five of us were watching, that old lady swung around and scuttled off across the grass. Ya, ya, on all fours, and believe me, no normal old lady can move her body that fast, okay? What's more, she passed right through the fence and went off into the lalang. You know how there used to be lalang growing wild behind the garden.

All of this happened. Not one word I've said is a lie.

Another strange thing was that Susanna told us later she wasn't the one who screamed. Not only that, she said she didn't hear any scream.

You see why I say there's only one explanation. But of course, not even Bernadette would admit it. She was the one to bring up my Rose after we were back in the dining room.

"Does Rose know anything about Shakilah's husband, yet?" she asked me, with her face still quite pale, but you see how she was pretending it was just a normal afternoon. Dorothy and Siew Chin also were sewing quietly. None of us were mentioning the old lady, and Susanna had already gone over to the church for her choir practice, since it was almost three o'clock. (I doubt-lah if that girl herself told anyone, except maybe Jo.)

You see how takut we were. Scared out of our wits-lah. We thought, in case the lady was you-know-who. Ya, it could have been the same lady as the bus drivers used to see, but that lady also could have been Pontianak, okay? Who's supposed to be beautiful beyond the imagination, true, but only when she appears to young men. Other times, you've heard the stories, right?

So I played along with Bernadette, knowing at the same time I had to be careful. "You know those two," I said. "Rose is not going to tell anyone Shakilah's business, okay? Their kind of friendship has deep roots, you know."

What went on between me and my daughter was my own business, ya? Of course I had tried to pry loose the actual story about what was what, umpteen times already. But that daughter of mine, like pulling teeth. And no-lah, I couldn't read her mind. People like to talk about mother's intuition, but it's nonsense, okay? You see my Rose. See how deep still waters can run.

Anyway, Dorothy joined in with her "I don't think there's a husband involved," which she had been saying ever since Shakilah came home, so it was nothing new.

"I don't think so, either," Bernadette said, which also was nothing new.

Only Siew Chin and I had been trying to give Shakilah the benefit of the doubt, although to be honest, in my heart, I actually agreed with Dorothy and Bernadette, and that could be the case with Siew Chin also. But someone had to come to the girl's rescue, ya? Only this afternoon, apparently, neither of us wanted to talk about Valerie and her daughter.

Siew Chin at that moment was stitching up a purple velvet sheath for the puppet that would be carrying a dagger. Without looking up, she changed the topic by asking, "Did Father Pereira tell anyone what the wayang is going to be about?"

Ya, ya, we already knew the teenagers were writing their own script. No wonder-lah, since none of them had ever turned a page of the Ramayana. That's young people for you. Probably, they didn't even know much about wayang kulit, which in olden times was a harvest celebration, okay? That's why the play used to begin at dusk and run until dawn—which was something else about it that would have made Father O'Hara object, and that, you can believe the teenagers knew. (In olden times, the play would begin on the last day of the padi harvest-lah, so after all that hard work, people could sit back and relax. Imagine how skillful the dalang had to be, ya? First of all, he had to hold everyone's attention the whole night. And then not only that, but since the audience would be sitting on both sides of the screen, he had to make sure the puppets' movements were absolutely precise. Ya-lah, the women would be sitting behind the stage and all they could see were the shadows on the screen. Obviously, men and women weren't allowed to sit together the whole night. But that was then-lah.)

Dorothy took the bait and said, "Some kind of love story, must be. That's all they're interested in, at their age."

"I wonder why they want a kris," Siew Chin said, and to be honest, she sounded as if really, she was wondering. She was even looking at the dagger that Bernadette had made for the puppet out of gold foil. It was lying in the center of the table, among the various arms and legs, and you see Bernadette's hidden talent. The dagger was so tiny, and yet so perfectly shaped.

"You think a love story can't have a kris in it?" I said, mostly to keep us from returning to the other topic-lah.

"Every love story must have an element of danger," Dorothy said, and of course I was surprised to hear her agreeing with me, for a change.

Bernadette looked at me with a certain expression in her eyes, as if expecting me to say something. Don't know what-lah, but when I said nothing, she also kept quiet. To this day, I don't know what she was thinking at that moment.

Then we heard Father Pereira's car outside, so definitely, our chance to talk about the old lady while the event was still fresh was over.

So that was that-lah.

BY THE WAY, you know what else about the Pauh Janggi? Malay folklore teaches us, on the island on which it grows, lives a giant crab that sleeps in a cove. Twice a day, the crab swims out into the sea and that's when the waters of the sea rush into the cove. And that's what makes the tides-lah, not only gravity. That's what has been giving us high tide and low tide, since the beginning of the world.

Think about it, okay?

NO ONE KNOWS-lah who actually made the call. But here's the truth. When the police came, they came with handcuffs. Ya, ya, people remember, whether or not they admit it. The way those handcuffs shone, when Willy Coleman was marched out to the police car. And that Ying Ying, she was nowhere to be seen. This was on the following Friday, exactly five weeks from the night Auntie Coco's sister went missing. (Sister Sylvia was down with the flu, so that's why I happened to be around to see all this.) No-lah, no ambulance arrived, so it couldn't have been that bad-lah. Only thing, Ying Ying didn't step out of the house for several days after that. Too embarrassed to show her face. Sending her son out to run errands for her. Ya, ya, the boy was home when the police came. Could be, he was the one who called.

You know only black magic can wield that sort of power, making some of us see or hear one thing, and others seeing or hearing something else. (And by the way, according to Rose, Adelaide's grandson was with her that first Friday night. You remember, Bernadette said she didn't see him outside the house, although I had heard from Winifred that he was there.)

Now here's the thing. What if the Pauh Janggi is actually that apple tree that's written about in the Book of Genesis? What if that's where we are? And that's why all our gates have dragons. Must sound a bit gila, but now you understand why I started changing my ways. Don't forget the parable of the wise and foolish maidens. Don't forget the bridegroom's words. Watch therefore, for you know neither the day nor the hour.

Could be, the Apocalypse has already begun, ya? And Benjamin Nair's death was only part of it.

 ROSE SIM

W HEN YOU OPEN a window between our world and
theirs, who knows which spirits might approach you.
You can't choose who comes to the window. That's what they
say. Had Auntie Coco opened the window herself, or was it
someone else? Perhaps even us, long ago when we used to visit
Che' Halimah, because Shak had talked me into it, you know.
But we would do it just for fun. Or perhaps the window was
open for good, ever since the Srivijaya and Majapahit women
had first bargained with the spirits.

Auntie Coco herself had never seemed to me to be the sort
to go dabbling in black magic. I was thinking this when Shak

said, "Mahani seems to think it's the only possible explanation," as she was trying to arrange the six pillows on her bed before sitting down, so they would give her back as much support as possible.

Almost four weeks had passed since that Friday night, and Shak's back was aching more and more every day. We were going for walks only once a week now, because definitely the heat was wearing her down.

I watched her struggling to get comfortable as she sat down. She tried pushing herself up against the pillows, and then turning her body slowly one way, then another way, then yet another way. I couldn't think of what to say to help, except offer to make her some hot ginger tea.

So I asked her, "How about some ginger tea?" even though her mother would have made the tea already, if indeed it could make Shak feel better.

She was home as usual, Shak's mother. I remember she was in the kitchen while we were upstairs, but I don't remember what she was doing. We had passed her on the stairs because she was going down as we were going up, and I had noticed she looked more tired than usual. So she and Shak must have had another quarrel, I thought, possibly about the baby's father, or about the baby's future. (She would give us privacy whenever I was there, Shak's mother. My mother, on the other hand, would have found all sorts of excuses to keep coming into the room if we had been at my house. Although as it turned out, she was at Holy Family that afternoon, making puppets for the wayang show being organized by the youth group to raise money for charity.)

"Thanks, Rose, but I don't think ginger tea would help right now," said Shak. She sighed. She had stopped moving about and was half-sitting, half-lying down, with her body turned a bit on her side, one pillow tucked between her knees, the rest piled up behind her.

"What can I do?" I asked her. "Tell me what I can do."

She smiled. Even with her figure lost for the time being, you could feel her charm, Shak. You could feel it when she smiled, that same charm that used to send the boys swooning around us, out on the dance floor. Swooning to the beat of the bossa nova, swaying against the samba, and no wonder. Imagine, with her fast hips and her eyes like Cadbury chocolate and her eyelashes, who could resist Shak? So I was sure the baby's father was already pining for her, whoever he was. Some numbskull fellow, who must have quarrelled with her when she had told him she was pregnant, who maybe had tried to talk her into getting rid of the baby, because he wasn't ready to become a father.

"I'm glad you're here, Rose."

I wanted to ask her why, why she was glad I was there. Instead, I just smiled as if I understood, which I've always regretted, but there you have it.

Shak looked at me and smiled again. Then she returned to the conversation we had been having about Auntie Coco and her sister. "So what do you think?" she asked. "What's your guess about what might have happened?"

"I don't know," I told her. "Quite frankly, I'm surprised Mahani brought up black magic."

She nodded, knowing exactly what I meant. "I was surprised, too. But time changes us, you know."

But I didn't think Mahani had changed that much. (She was another librarian who used to attend St. Agnes, and since she and I worked together, I should know, right? Mahani was the one who used to tell our classmates, all those bomoh stories we were hearing were old wives' tales. *An idle mind is the devil's workshop, okay?* was what she would go around saying, although there was that incident that had happened when we were in Primary Two. One of our classmates, her name escapes me now, a girl from the same kampong as Mahani. Her father was dying of cancer when one day, the cancer disappeared and never came back. We thought it was a miracle at first, wrought by our prayers, perhaps. But shortly after the father was cured, the girl's mother was spotted in a shopping center, and people couldn't believe how much she had aged. They say that sort of thing can happen when you use black magic, if you have nothing else to pay with, if you're so poor, the only asset you can offer in exchange is your youth. No one knew if it was what the mother had resorted to, but certainly the possibility was there.)

I must admit, I was slightly taken aback to hear that Mahani had come over to visit Shak on her own, since I saw her almost every day at the library, and she had never mentioned it to me. But then, Mahani and I weren't friends, exactly. She wasn't friends with Chandra, either, which I was glad about, now that I knew. Not that I disliked Mahani in any way, you know. It wasn't because of that, that we weren't friends.

But I've always liked my privacy, and privacy's not easy to come by in Singapore. It never was.

"How did Mahani hear about Auntie Coco's sister?" I asked. (Of course what I wanted to know was what else the two of them had talked about, but I thought, sooner or later, Shak would tell me on her own. And it was better that way.)

"Oh, you know." Shak was looking at me a bit wistfully, so I wondered if she was thinking about the doctor's son again. We hadn't talked about it since that Friday, although there were moments I could feel her wanting to throw things into the open. Other times, it seemed as if she was becoming more like me, leaving the past alone. We hadn't even talked about the morning Laura Timmerman had looked out of the bathroom window while she was uncapping the tube of toothpaste, and there was the doctor's son, tied to one of the rambutan trees. Naked again. Or about what the doctor's servant had seen, the one who was sent out to untie the boy.

An old lady squatting overhead in the treetop, whom the boy himself claimed he couldn't see. No one had ever known what to make of it.

"I think it's too early to tell," I said. "For all we know, even as we speak, someone may have found the sister and is taking her to the police station right now."

"You don't really believe that, Rose."

"I know. But you remember how people here will gossip without knowing anything. You remember?"

"Yes, I do remember."

Already, everyone could feel the sister was gone for good. As if somehow, she was already just one more shadow when the sun rose, just one more leaf dropping off the trees. (Auntie Coco must have known it also. She especially. She seldom came out of her house now, and those of the neighbors who had tried to visit her were saying she wouldn't even come out to the gate or answer the telephone.)

On the wall above Shak's bed, the pattern of the window railing disappeared briefly, then appeared again. The same pattern as would show up on my bedroom wall, because all of our houses had the same railing, to prevent children from tumbling out and cracking their heads open.

It must have been around half-past two, although something felt later. We had gone upstairs after lunch, I remember. I could smell the lime blossoms drifting up to us from Shak's back garden. So familiar, the way her room smelled, as if here, nothing could ever be ruined, or changed. Because see how Shak was snuggling against the headboard with her pillows, facing me where I was, at the foot of the bed just like years ago. We would sit like that, our voices weaving together as we talked, our hearts locking in the embrace of children's hearts. That was Shak and me. The way we used to be, before anything had happened.

Perhaps it was why at the time, I didn't pay attention to the missing photographs. Because at that moment, who cared why of all things to remove from her room, her mother had chosen to remove the photographs of Shak's father? There used to be two, you know, up there on her bureau beside the bed. Those were the only things missing from the room. The other photographs were still there, I remember, those of Shak alone, or Shak with her mother, or Shak with her aunties on her mother's side, and there was one with Shak's grandmother, which had been taken outside the grandmother's house, back when everyone was still in touch.

See how life is when your best friend comes home, never mind whether or not she will stay for good, and never mind her swollen feet and the watermelon.

Even with Auntie Coco's misfortune lingering in the air, I felt oddly happy.

"Hey, Rose?"

When I looked away from the railing pattern on the wall, Shak was eying me as if she knew exactly how I was feeling. But all she asked was, "Do people still talk about the diamond woman?"

"Sometimes," I said, "but not much."

Because it was true. Although the story still came up now and then, most of us had gone around it several times already. And I wasn't fond of that story myself, you know. I remember, when Shak and I had first heard about it, for days, I wasn't able to look at my own father directly. I'll admit, I was glad when people's attention wandered elsewhere.

"So people still don't know who she was," Shak murmured.

"No," I said. "No one knows."

She sighed, and I watched her tired face. Of course I wanted to tell her how much I had missed her. But why talk about what we cannot change?

"Have you talked to Isabella about it?" Shak asked, returning again to Auntie Coco and her sister.

"No," I said, and then I thought I might as well tell her I hadn't seen Isabella since that Friday at the library. (She had asked me then, Isabella, whether I knew she would be leaving for America soon, and of course I had heard about it. She was going over for further studies in psychology at the University of Chicago, something like that. She had invited me to her farewell luncheon at the convent, and I had said yes, even though I knew I wouldn't be able to bring myself to do it. I was surprised Shak hadn't asked me about it, but for some reason, we hadn't talked about Isabella until now. Although I knew Isabella had come to visit her, as she had said she would.)

"You didn't see her before she left?" Shak asked, after I had told her. She sounded genuinely surprised, which surprised me, because I thought after talking with Isabella, she would know how Isabella and I didn't see much of each other.

"We're not that close, you know," I said. "You guys were friends, but she and I, you know how it is, as time passes, and we all end up with our own lives."

She and Shak, you know, in those two years while they were on the team. Always laughing over something. Sitting on the wet tiles at the edge of the pool with their feet kicking up water, bending their heads together so they could whisper about the coach, or about the other girls, or about boys. Back then, it may have made me a bit jealous, I don't remember if it did or not. But I always knew, it was only because I wasn't on the team that Shak and Isabella became buddy buddy in that way.

Shak was looking at me, as if waiting for an answer.

"What?" I asked.

She shook her head and started smacking a pillow. "Mrs. Sandhu's been asking about you," she said.

"Asking what?"

"She just wanted to know how you were. She says she never runs into you. She was under the impression you had migrated somewhere."

I watched Shak shoving the pillow wearily beneath her right breast, her hair falling like a wave over her face.

"I'd forgotten how humid it can get." She sighed, pushing her hair back from her face. "Mrs. Sandhu's thinking of selling her house, moving into a smaller place. You know her husband's passed away?"

I nodded, having read the obituary when it happened.

"Remember how when we were in school, every now and then he would send a bouquet of roses with the chauffeur when the chauffeur came to pick her up?" Shak had lain back and closed her eyes, a smile on her lips.

"You used to refer to him as Mr. Sandhu Charming," I said. "And once, Mrs. Sandhu heard you."

"Yes, she did." Shak was still smiling, her face relaxing in a way I hadn't seen since she had come home. "Aren't you sleepy, Rose?"

"I'm used to the heat," I said. "You go ahead and rest, okay?"

She nodded, then asked, "Will you watch for the dragons?"

"Yes," I said, as if we were still children. "I'll watch for the dragons."

She patted her womb and whispered, "Rose will watch for the dragons," to the baby. (You know they say even in the womb, babies can feel the world around them, can pick up on feelings, that sort of thing.)

I must have been sleepier than I realized, because I don't remember closing my eyes. One moment, I was watching Shak's face while she slept. The next moment, I was waking up with my right cheek resting on my right arm, my torso stretched out sideways across the blue-and-white paisley sheet, and she was watching me.

SHAK SAID SHE had been awake only a few minutes before I opened my eyes. She was looking less tired as she sat at the dressing table, brushing her hair. I had moved up from the foot of the bed and was sitting near the pillows, watching her, trying to seize every minute, since I didn't know how long more she would be around.

We hadn't talked about when she was planning to go back to America. When Shak had first arrived, she had said only that she wasn't back for good. But she wanted to see how things went, with her mother especially, before she thought about when to leave.

So I didn't want to ask her about it, in case talking made it happen, somehow. And yet, deep down inside, I must have known she could never settle here. Not now. Because Singaporeans who go to England or Australia, they often return, you know, but the ones who've gone to America, they seldom come back. (With Isabella, it would have to be different, I thought. Because of her vows.)

Shak's dress was aquamarine that afternoon, beautiful as a kingfisher feather. And the sun, I remember, was coming through the window on her left and flying off her hair.

"So, what if Auntie Coco's sister left of her own free will?" she said, still facing the mirror. "Unless you're tired of talking about it. Are you?" Shak glanced at me, and I shook my head.

"What do you mean?" I asked, although I could tell from her tone, she was thinking of Che' Halimah. So I knew she had heard a rumor that was only just starting, about how Che' Halimah may have coaxed Auntie Coco's sister over to her house. Because Che' Halimah was getting old, and it was time for her to start training an apprentice.

So the rumor went. And as I've said, it was only just starting. Not even my mother knew about it, you know. Because being of her generation, my mother wasn't paying attention to certain conversations. And it's true. Some things, only those who are silent most of the time, only they can hear.

"Do you think the police have been to Kampong Alam?" Shak asked, putting down her brush.

"Probably," I replied, although I didn't know for certain.

"But they didn't visit every house."

Might as well get to the point, I thought, so I said, "You think Auntie Coco's sister is in the bomoh's house?"

"She could be. It's probably the one place nobody's looked."

"Our police are quite thorough, you know. Anyway, how could Auntie Coco's sister make her way through the cemetery on her own?"

"She wouldn't have had to do it on her own, Rose." Shak got up and stepped over to the bed.

I moved back to my old position at the foot of the bed, so she could sit with her pillows again.

"You don't think it's possible? Rose?"

"You think the beggar was here to guide her to the house?" I was referring to the old fellow some neighbors were saying might be involved in Auntie Coco's sister's disappearance, but only because he was a stranger and had shown up in our neighborhood so suddenly. I myself hadn't seen him. Neither had Shak, as far as I knew.

"Oh, I hadn't thought of that. But sure, maybe. That would be one way. But Che' Halimah has other ways, you know."

But still, why would Che' Halimah have chosen a retarded woman? I pointed it out to Shak, as if she wouldn't have thought about it already. "Auntie Coco's sister is retarded," I reminded her.

"What if she's really not?"

"I'm sure she is, Shak."

"You are?"

"Yes."

That was when Shak reached for my hand, and I felt the smoothness of the emeralds as she slid the bracelet into my palm. "A close friend gave this to me," she said, out of the blue, just like that. "I want to give it to you. Okay?"

All I could do was nod. I should have wondered then and there, why she was giving it to me. And also, why she seemed so certain the rumor about Auntie Coco's sister was true. But the way she had said *a close friend* was stuck like a thorn in my heart, and it was all I could think about at that moment.

Which close friend? Was it Mahani? Isabella? Why didn't she want to tell me who it was? I wanted to ask, but now Shak was sitting there with both hands on her womb, fingertips to fingertips, and she was gazing down and smiling, as if she could see right through her hands, through her dress, through her abdomen, directly into her baby. As if she was smiling into her baby, to fill the baby with her whole self, that was how it was.

So I didn't want to disturb her.

Only I found myself wondering more than ever, what her baby was going to look like, since I still knew nothing about the father. And if the baby turned out to have blond hair and blue eyes, then what? Of course it mattered to me, whether or not the baby would look like Shak.

Not anymore, but at the time, it mattered.

"IT'S A SHRINE." Shak told me, when she showed me the red matchbox with the picture of a couple holding hands painted onto it. She had pulled out the matchbox drawer to show me what was inside also—a doll with long black hair, wearing a yellow dress, a plastic capsule like a big pill capsule, and a strip of white paper.

"A shrine," I repeated, and then I asked her, "What religion?" since I had never seen a shrine like that.

"Catholic," she said, smiling because she could tell from my expression, I didn't know whether or not she was joking.

It was almost half-past five, the sun sloping gently across the bed. Shak was showing me some things she wanted me to see before I left that evening, and what comes back to me now is her voice. Shak's voice, the sound of it, even with her accent, making me think of ink flowing on rice paper. Of a whisper blowing on your skin, like that.

Outside, there was a rattling in the lime trees, and we could hear birds squawking in the garden.

"Really, it's Catholic," Shak said, with some amusement in her voice, and when I didn't say anything, she thought for a moment and then she added, "All right, it's not Vatican Catholic. More like folk Catholic. See this?" She pointed to the plastic capsule and I looked. Déjà vu, the two of us like that, both examining something together, in those bygone days when the world used to be so fresh, and everything we collected from it was a novelty. "It's holy dirt. Sort of like holy water, you know? It's from a sanctuary in New Mexico, where they say miracles have happened for people who've gone there to pray."

Shak could tell I didn't understand, probably from the way I didn't want to admit it.

"It's Mexican-American folk religion, Rose. Catholic, from a Mexican-American point of view. Know what I mean?" She sighed, and I wondered if she was about to give up, so I searched for something to say. Sometimes what you have to do is just keep talking, right?

So I said, "Mexican?"

"Mexican-American. It's not the same thing, over there. I mean, it's not the same thing." She sighed again. "There's a lot about American history we never learned, you know, Rose? Did you know the slaves used to kill their babies to protect them from the masters? The women. Can you imagine it? Killing your own baby to protect it?"

"Murder is a sin," was all I could think to say, even though I had watched the whole series of *Roots*, you know.

"Oh, Rose." Shak shook her head at me, eying me as if to say, *Don't be a dumkopf.* "It's not that simple. Mothers have to protect their children. All right, think about this. What if your husband's abusing your child? Say, if he's a drunk and beats up on the child, or does worse things, and the police don't believe you, or if you live in a country where are no laws against something like that. There are such places, you know. What would you do?"

I looked at the shrine that was from that sanctuary where miracles were granted, even if it was American. And I asked for something to say, but no help came to me. Obviously Shak was trying to get me to understand something very important to her, later when she showed me the other things also. Some postcards she had brought over from America, and her photographs from there. I knew she was searching for a way to explain why she had stayed away so long, why she had come back now, maybe even why I would never see her again after this, as if she could answer something like that. Of course I didn't know, yet, what was going to happen. All I knew was that Shak didn't fit in among us anymore. Of course I had noticed it, how she didn't seem as happy as when she had first arrived, as if her life in America was starting to call her back, her heart missing someone there in a way she had never missed me.

There were no photographs of that numbskull fellow, only of Shak's apartment, and her tropical plants. All her rooms had plants in them, which was something I hadn't known about Shak before, that she loved plants. There was even a hibiscus, imagine, which her friend Celia was watering in the photograph.

This was the friend who was taking care of her plants while she was away. Shak must have called out to her, "Hey, turn around," and her friend had turned around and smiled, quite impromptu. (She was very pretty, and also I noticed she looked mixed.)

Shak may have been waiting for me to do it, but I couldn't bring myself to ask her who the baby's father was.

The last thing she showed me that afternoon was a piece of her writing, which she said she had found while cleaning out the drawers in her wardrobe. The writing was on ruled paper, with the sentences not staying on the lines. The words had a blurry look because the ink must have melted a bit over the years. I recognized Shak's younger handwriting at once, her splashing loops and lanky, daring strokes.

After I had read the piece, she said, "I don't remember it. I was probably still half-asleep."

"You used to write down your dreams," I said, which was true. But she had never shown me the recorded dreams because her writing used to be very private to her.

"Yes, I did." She smiled. "I still do, sometimes."

I didn't ask her about the dream in the writing, and Shak didn't say anything else about it. All she did was ask whether I wanted to keep the piece.

I told her yes.

She didn't ask me why, and she never would. Nor would she tell me about the will she was making, or that she was going to more or less bequeath her baby to Evelina Thumboo, of all people. All that, I wouldn't find out until later, after everything was over, so to speak.

THIS WAS WHAT Shak had written down:

> *Violent sex dreams. I'm across the road. I hear two girls learning about sex? in the house. My parents are in the house. The girls come out because they made a mistake and got fired. My parents go on playing. Later I hear my mother screaming. My father wants to play the bye-bye game. My mother screams, begs, No. My father goes to the door, opens it, says bye-bye, closes the door. But he doesn't come out. It's only a starting point. Once he closes the door, there's no going back. My mother screams and screams. I rattle my fingers in my ears to drown out the screams.*
>
> *Something about two boxes. I think they put on these boxes over their heads and walk around the room. If they bump into each other, he fucks her. It's violent. He uses knives. One is a metal spatula. She has 28 scars in 10 days. I'm crying. If she gets 28 more, she'll die.*

Outside the house, my father says we must talk. I follow him back across the road. I don't think he will hurt me but he's drunk. A policeman, a friend, a wimpy sort of guy, comes with us and tries to take my father to jail.

Underneath the dream, she had added:

My father in this dream looks different. Rougher. He doesn't look like my dad in real life.

I couldn't make heads or tails of it at the time, and Shak must have known this. But she must have known also, when she gave it to me, that I would read it again and again. She must have known I would keep trying, because she knew me.

 TWO LISTENERS

FATIMAH AZIZ

daughter of rohana binte aziz, a.k.a. kechil

father unknown

WHAT MY MOTHER'S friends say about the widow Valerie Nair is that, for over a decade, she was brewing medicine with her husband's coffee, scooping the ground leaves into the aluminum decanter before adding coffee powder. And so morning after morning her husband had grown weaker, his bones wilting so slowly, he himself didn't notice until it was too late. By the time the symptoms of illness were unmistakable, his bones were almost hollow, his muscle barely attached, his blood a turbid brown like cheap ordinary tea, so that not even the smartest doctors could save him.

This was what happened long before we were born, back

when Che' Halimah was alive and living in the Chinese bomoh's house, which itself is about to go. (No one ever calls the Chinese bomoh by name, or understands why Che' Halimah broke the tradition of choosing a kampong girl to take over when she grew ill.) My mother's friends say, the Chinese bomoh's medicine is only so-so, but my mother tells me it's good enough and that people have to stop asking for the moon. She says they'll all regret complaining when the bomoh's house gets torn down (the government's been warning for years that kampongs are fire hazards, what with all those atap roofs). Our kampong's the last to go, and who knows what will happen then? That's how my mother says it. *Our kampong*, she says, even though we don't live there, and I never have. But my grandfather lives there, and my mother and my Uncle Abdul grew up there, so I say it, too, because Maria tells me it's true—our kampong will be demolished soon. And she says *your kampong* because she and I are closer than sisters, and we know each other. We don't know how Maria knows what will happen before it does, but she's always right.

It may be that Maria was born with a veil, although Auntie Eve says she wasn't, and Auntie Eve was in the room at the time. (Malika wasn't. Maria says Malika came to live with them a few days after, so she's not the one to ask.) My mother says there are women who believe babies born with the veil bring bad luck, and that Auntie Eve may not remember because she's superstitious and doesn't understand. But Auntie Eve's memory seems fine to me, and anyone can see Maria's the precious jewel of her heart. But it may be that Maria was born with a veil, and Auntie Eve doesn't want to say it out loud (in case a spirit passing by hears).

We don't talk about this, Maria and I. We don't talk about her birth, or about her mother. It's the only thing we don't talk about, the night of her birth the only closed door between us.

So when the widow approached us at the church yesterday, I didn't know how to warn her. Maria doesn't know what I know.

She doesn't know about Auntie Eve's old neighbors and their secret acts, or why Auntie Eve moved away, because when my mother's friends at the kampong talk, there are things they don't tell outsiders. And even though Maria and I have known each other our whole lives, she's still an outsider to them.

"Girl, what's your name?" the widow asked, and when we turned around, she was looking at Maria, her irises dark and turbulent like a nightmare.

That was how I knew it was her, the one who had gone so far as to murder her husband by the only untraceable means. I had never seen her before yesterday, because Maria and I don't live in that neighborhood and we don't go to that church. We don't go to any church, although Auntie Eve's Catholic and so's Maria. (Sometimes they attend Mass at a church near the Christian cemetery, when they visit Maria's mother's grave, but otherwise, Auntie Eve likes to keep priests and nuns and anyone holy at arm's length, as she puts it.) Maria and I wouldn't have been there yesterday if Maria hadn't decided to join the youth choir, if our classmate Lucinda Tan hadn't asked us, which had happened not because Lucinda wants to be friends, I know, but because Maria's voice is strong and sweeter than cotton candy in our mouths, and I should have guessed, too, what Lucinda didn't tell us but Maria knew, that Derek Ashley's in the choir.

That was why we were in the foyer, at the bottom of the spiral staircase leading up to the choir loft, at one o'clock when the widow was there. There was no one else in the pews, and no sign of the other choir members because Lucinda Tan had given us the wrong time, telling us choir practice would start at half-past one, forgetting it was starting later yesterday because the choir mistress was dropping her friend off at the airport on the way.

What Maria knows about the widow is what Auntie Eve's old neighbors tell anyone who asks, that there was once a falling out between the widow and her grown-up daughter, that this falling out was the reason the widow's daughter migrated to

America in the first place. The widow's daughter didn't return for fifteen years, and when she did, it was to give birth to the widow's granddaughter, conceived out of wedlock and delivered dead in the widow's house. No wonder the widow lost her mind. This is how Auntie Eve's old neighbors put it. They never saw the widow's daughter again after that night, which is why some say she probably died, too, shortly after giving birth. Others say they're sure the widow's daughter's gone back to America, and is living in New York City and doing well, teaching in a university over there, all things considered.

That's what they say, and no one mentions the sticks tied to the widow's fence the night the daughter was giving birth. My mother's friends say it was Sister Rosalind's mother's idea (whom we've never seen visiting Sister Rosalind at school—Maria says why would her mother come, Sister Rosalind won't talk to anyone and not even to the other nuns, which is true—Sister Rosalind mostly stays in her room, although some nights on retreat, or so we hear, girls have seen her sitting in the lime orchard, her back all straight on the stone bench, her gaze fixed far ahead in the distance, as if someone were coming towards her or as if Sister Rosalind's caught up remembering when someone was). My mother's friends say it took Sister Rosalind's mother over an hour to arrange the sticks, because they had to be tied straight, with all the sharp ends pointing up, an even row of makeshift swords to pierce Pontianak's belly, should she venture to fly over and try to steal the baby. But Sister Rosalind's mother wasn't in the room when the baby was born, because although she was a neighbor, she wasn't close to the widow like family.

They say it's sheer coincidence this happened exactly twelve years ago, in 1994 when Maria was born, a year before me. (The lady Coco Han's sister disappeared that year, too). Maria's never wondered as I have, why no one knows where the baby's buried, or if a funeral was even held. Auntie Eve says the baby was taken away in an ambulance, and I don't ask her much else, because I know she knows Maria and I don't talk about this, and I won't betray Maria.

But Auntie Eve knows, too, about Maria's dreams, and she knows I know. (Maria says it's always the same girl calling her over to the sugar cane. She says the girl's trying to make her see something, but all Maria ever remembers is the girl's bracelet sliding down her wrist, a string of green stones. She says whenever she tries to walk over to the girl, she wakes up. Malika knows about these dreams as well. You can tell Malika knows from the way she watches Maria. But Malika doesn't speak much, and I swear she must be a hundred years old and whacko-crazy, but Maria loves Malika, so I don't say anything about it.)

I had noticed the widow as soon as Maria and I were in the church, as she was the only other person there. She was over at the candles, and I thought she was just some Catholic lady, kneeling before one of the tall marble statues along the left wall (of St. Anthony, I found later, who's the patron saint of lost things), and she had seemed to be praying so intently, gazing up at the statue as if it were the saint himself, his face benevolent in the flickering light. So I wasn't on guard. Maria and I had our backs to her when she came up to us. We were facing the church doors, watching for the other choir members to arrive.

Before I could stop her, Maria was telling the widow her name.

"Maria Thumboo," she said, her voice echoing fearlessly in the foyer.

The widow smiled, and I could see it in her face that she recognized Maria, even though they had never met. I could see she knew who Maria was, who she is, and that I've been right all along.

HER HUSBAND USED to go after young girls. They're saying the widow had always suspected his nature, but before she had married this man, she had loved him madly and allowed herself a moment's indiscretion, telling herself he felt the same, and she wouldn't admit he was marrying her only for her family's money, which they say remains her money even though her family's cut her off. That happened when the family found out about my Auntie Bettina, when my grandmother told them. My mother was four when my Auntie Bettina was raped, and my auntie herself was only fifteen. That was when the widow should have known she had averted her eyes long enough, but my mother says she wouldn't face the fact her husband would never change, until the day she found her own daughter bleeding on her bed.

This, too, was long before Maria and I were born, before even my Uncle Abdul was born, and before the robbery in which almost everyone in our family would be slaughtered like pigs. My mother says my Auntie Bettina was working as a hotel maid at the Goodwood, to help the family make ends meet, because we were poor and my auntie was the eldest daughter. She says the widow's husband was waiting for my auntie when she got off the bus that night, but my auntie didn't know she was being waylaid, because the widow's husband was handsome and charming, and he was a neighbor, and he was a father with a baby daughter at home. They had spoken before, so when he offered to walk her back to the kampong, she accepted, won over by his good looks and his charm but also because it was past midnight and she was often afraid, walking home by herself.

He raped her near the tadpole pond, halfway between the kampong compound and the road. My auntie was in such shock, she walked home after that without putting her clothes back on (later, my mother would have to accompany her second eldest sister, my Auntie Noi, to the pond to retrieve the muddied blue dress and torn white panties). My mother was the first to notice my Auntie Bettina appearing out of the trees. She had woken up to pee and happened to be outside. There was a full moon, she says, and she watched her sister stepping out of the trees as naked as an animal, and when my auntie came closer, my mother saw the blood on her legs and that was when she screamed.

No one heard the widow scream when she found her daughter, but it was what made her give in, in the end, that sweep of excruciating shame and loss of face and unabated fury. Some time had passed since my grandmother had spoken to the widow's family, and then on a rainy November night, when the air was especially potent and sweet, the widow was seen coming down the steps outside Che' Halimah's house. My mother remembers the frangipani around the house glowing that night as if the flowers were tiny lanterns, about the size of children's hands.

She says I'm almost too young to hear all this, but old enough because I look older than I am, she says, because I'm tall for my age, and my breasts are developing, and I'm pretty.

Not as pretty as Maria, though. I know Maria's prettier, even though Maria worries about how flat she is, because Maria's seen my breasts when we shower. Even if beauty's in the eye of the beholder, I feel Maria's prettiness. I feel it in my heart's unreeling at the sight of her, faster than a fish line hooked to a shark heading for deep water when she touches me, when she touches my breast to know how touching a breast feels. I feel it, and sometimes I think I want to kiss her. But sometimes I just want to look at her. Sometimes when we're sitting side by side, doing nothing but just talking, my heart flies like a kite let loose so high up in the sky it has become invisible, and all that's left is the fine thread tugging at me in the wind.

My mother and I don't talk about Maria anymore, these days, not since she found out about Maria's dreams. Her face bangs shut whenever I say Maria's name, as if there's something there she would rather I not know. So I don't tell her how Derek Ashley's breaking my heart even though he hasn't yet seen Maria, because they haven't exactly met, not yet, but they will, because Maria's got it planned, and I know when they do, he'll fall for her, head over heels, even if she's flatter than a pancake right now, which is how Maria puts it.

Because she won't be for long, and it isn't true that she's even as flat as she thinks. I've felt the bumps on Maria's chest, the rise around her nipples, which are softer than the rest of her at first, then wrinkle like raisins, just like mine.

Maybe that was what made it possible for the widow to catch us by surprise. Because my attention was on Maria the whole time and she hadn't told me she had found out about Derek Ashley's being in the choir, and I was looking in the other direction and puzzling over why she would want us to waste every Saturday afternoon in a church, among those mournful marble statues and eerie white candles, with the prayers of the sick and lonely Catholics hanging over our heads like curses. (There seem to be a lot of sick and lonely people among the Catholics, and sometimes I wonder if it's because they're not allowed to visit a bomoh or believe in reincarnation, only in heaven and hell and purgatory, and because all Catholics get sent to purgatory first, no matter what they do. Or so it seems, because we're always offering prayers for them during Assembly at St. Agnes, after we've sung the National Anthem and recited the Pledge.)

Whatever the reason for my inattentiveness, I was there with Maria, and my mother says we're responsible for every life that shares our path in this world, whether it's the life of a plant or an animal or another human being.

But that's not why I did it.

BECAUSE MARIA WAS wearing her new perfume yesterday and her skin was fragrant when we were in the foyer, fragrant like jasmine in the dark, like pandan leaves when it rains, like the world when we're listening to it from inside the cemetery (where we're not supposed to go, but what my mother and

Auntie Eve don't know can't hurt us, and Maria agrees with me on this). That was why, and my heart knows it. But if Auntie Eve asks, I'm going to say it's because I recognized the widow, and she found out Maria's name, and I knew Maria might be in danger because that must have been why Auntie Eve had kept the truth from her all these years. I'll say that's why I decided to tell her, because I wasn't ready when the widow came up to us and Maria had already given the widow her name.

I didn't mean to tell Maria everything, just who Valerie Nair really was. I decided I would just say it.

"She's your grandmother," I said. "And she's crazy."

This was about five minutes later, after I had managed to get Maria away from the widow, and we were still at the church but outside, on the steps. There was still no sign of the choir members. I could feel the breeze sweeping down through the fan palms across the church driveway, and on the road, a few cars passed with sunlight bouncing off their rearview mirrors. We were on the Changi Road side of the church, so I knew at least some of the choir members would be coming from the other side, the Siglap Hill side, where the car park is, and the parish house. (So I didn't think we might be there at the wrong time, because some of the members could have arrived already and might be hanging out in the parish house.)

Maria thought I was joking, at first. She laughed and pushed me in her playful way, and said, "You're the crazy one."

"I'm not joking," I said. "That's why you don't know. She killed your grandfather, okay? She used black magic on him. That's why you were adopted by your Auntie Eve, to hide you from your crazy grandmother."

Maria already knew she was adopted, and I knew she knew, even though we don't talk about that. So I wasn't hurting her feelings. But I hadn't meant to tell her about what the widow had done, and I didn't know until the words were out of my mouth that I would say all that.

She stared at me as if I had just slapped her face, as if I had slapped her hard, as I would never do.

You can't take your words back once they're out. You can't, so I just looked at her and hoped she would say something, anything, to let me know what to say next.

"Why are you saying that?" she asked, her voice lowering to a hush, shaky with disbelief.

I shrugged my shoulders. I felt miserable, but I still thought if I could get Maria to believe me, and believe that we had to leave the church immediately, since the widow was still inside, then she might even change her mind about joining the choir. Then she and I could go do what we usually do on Saturdays and Sundays. We could ride the bus to Ocean Theatre and see a cheap matinee, or window-shop at Katong Shopping Center and try on new jeans at Bibi and Baba and read the new T-shirt slogans, or we could cycle to Marine Parade and feed bread crumbs to the fish weaving about in the water in the lagoon, and walk in the waves on the beach, and sit on the sand, side by side, and talk into the sunset, with our arms and elbows rubbing, and her perfume blowing in the saltwater breeze.

But Maria looked at me a long time, and then she said, calmly, "I'm going to ask my Auntie Eve if you're lying."

And I saw her expression had changed, and I knew there was no way she would change her mind about the choir. I knew it even before she turned and stepped back into the church, without looking to see if I would follow her.

That was yesterday.

Today I'm remembering watching Maria as she disappeared into the dim foyer, slipping in between the church doors. I'm remembering her shoulders, and the curve of her arms in her sleeveless white blouse with the tiny lace collar and the five tiny buttons shaped like starfish down her back.

My heart is falling as if it will never stop. Somewhere far inside me, it just falls and falls, without making a sound.

EVE THUMBOO

daughter of aloysius and rita kim

(both deceased)

adoptive mother of maria

WHAT I REMEMBER about that morning is the moonlight, slipping so white through the branches of the jacaranda onto the cement floor of the hotel room balcony, and the air smelling sweet like a rebirth, like freedom. Dawn at the edges of my mind, but nowhere around us that I could see, for outside were only the dark fields and groves of trees furrowed so prettily by the moonlight, and the kampong, hidden by the trees, where the boy who had set up the meeting for me was sleeping, and the river, a black ribbon winding through the moonlight, in which the kampong families bathed and washed their things and where their sewer water emptied, all into the same river. Not that I had asked the boy about it. All I had asked him was how well he knew the man who was going to handle the whole thing—I wanted to know if he was trustworthy, of course. The man, I mean, not the boy. I trusted the boy, perhaps because he was still a boy, no older than fourteen or fifteen, I would think. My brother's age, or the age my brother would have been (the doctors couldn't explain what made him stop breathing six months after he was born, except to say some-times that sort of thing happened)—"He's my uncle," the boy had said to me in answer to my question, and then he had added, "You want to know what I'm going to do with the money?" And that was when he had told me about the kampong and how we rich Singaporeans were spoiled, complaining about hardship when we had never tasted true hardship. And then he had apologized, of course—I think he may have had a slight crush on me. But he could also see I was genuinely distressed, because I was. You didn't get that sort of information from brochures, or from history books for that matter, in those days. And I was only twenty-three, and still very unexposed.

Not that the boy was trying to get me to change my mind—why would he? He wanted the money. But if there had been a moment when I could have turned back, it would have been that moment, while he was talking about the kampong and I wondered, briefly only, if I myself was asking for too much. So why didn't I turn back? Was your Auntie Eve born with evil already in her soul?

You will have to decide, my darling.

IT WAS ALVIN who had booked our room. Cameron Highlands was one of his haunts, you see, ever since he was a boy. I, on the other hand, had never left Singapore before our honeymoon. Anywhere else he could have chosen for us to go, I would have been as much of a stranger as I was at that hotel, so the locale didn't matter. And the room they had given us was lovely, very modern, very clean, and as the hotel was on a slope, we had that view of the countryside that I was admiring in the moonlight on the morning I was to meet the boy's uncle.

I was on the balcony only a few minutes. Someone may have seen me, but what would anyone have thought? Just another rich man's wife, or his daughter, who was having trouble sleeping. And if another woman had seen me? She may have suspected more, but I wouldn't think it would have been enough. If a woman had seen me, she herself might have been some tycoon's wife or daughter, staying at the hotel on holiday with her family. Unless she was a prostitute, or one of the maids . . . Not that this possibility of being noticed or recognized had even entered my mind, of course. Not that I had much of a plan, you see. Nor would anyone step forward later to say that he or she had seen me on the balcony around four o'clock that morning, or that shortly after that, he or she had seen a woman leaving the hotel by herself and walking off in the direction of the kampong and the river, carrying a small bundle by her side, too large to be a purse and too small to be any kind of food sack, the kind of bundle you might make from a wide silk scarf, for instance, if your purse couldn't hold all the dollar notes you needed to take with you. Not that I was ever at risk of getting caught, because Halimah's medicine was undetectable.

Are you sure you want to hear more? Now you've gone and kachaued whomever you could find, are you at all closer to the truth? You must decide, that's right.

All right, then. Bring that candle over here, and close your eyes. Because the truth, my darling, is seldom the first thing we see, but the dust of conversations, floating in breath, just out of sight.

HE WAS WAITING for me underneath the banyan tree, just as the boy had promised. Wearing a white songkok like a haji, a white kurta, and white trousers, moonlight swaying at his feet as the banyan leaves shook at my approach. No shoes. I could draw you his face, but what would be the point? He may not look the same anymore, and if years from now you want to go looking for him, if you feel you must, remember what he may be, for the boy may have lied to me, and he, being of that certain nature, can change his face, become a woman if he wants to, even return as a child, as Pontianak, as his daughter.

You follow what I'm saying? Once you ask, it's only polite to listen, follow the spaces between our words, surrender. Otherwise, don't ask.

Yes, bring another candle, and check the latch on that window over there, please. A wind is about to come. Hear how the birds are holding their breath.

SO, HE WAS waiting for me underneath the banyan tree. Because of the way he looked at me, and the raw hunger in his voice when he asked, "Where is your husband now?" as if I weren't the one paying him, even with my inexperience, I was already wondering if the boy had lied, if perhaps I had been lured into their trap, if I was in danger. But then I remembered Halimah. She would have warned me, so since she hadn't, I became unafraid, only remaining wary.

Yes, of course I felt disappointed with the boy, disappointed because there was something cannibalistic in the man's smile when he unbuttoned my blouse with his eyes, his teeth like a razor on my throat. Even if he was the boy's uncle, the boy had lied to me in another way, you see, and because he was the age my brother would have been, because I was so innocent, because right up to my wedding day, I had been allowed out only with my amahs (my mother, you remember, died giving birth to my brother), I wanted to believe boys were not like men, that at fourteen or fifteen, a boy had not yet become my husband, or other women's husbands, or my father. But I could not idle the morning away, feeling disappointed. I had business to take care of, and dawn was just over the horizon, a vague lightening of the sky beyond the river, a purplish tint in the shadows around us.

"Where is your husband now?" the man asked again.

Somewhere I couldn't see, a rooster had begun to crow.

Yes, I remember his voice. I will always remember his voice, and I remember how I answered the question. "Sleeping." Flatly, without background, not like a wife or a daughter or a mistress, and not even like a servant or an amah. I said it as if Alvin weren't my husband, as if I were a hotel maid who cleaned his room, or one of those immigrant girls removing trays from a table he had sat at in a hawker center. I spoke as if he were a passing customer, with a stranger's face like the faces of other customers, hair, nose, eyes, mouth, cheekbones, nothing to make him stand out, nothing to endear him to me. As if I myself had crumbled into sand, chips of granite, filaments of rain now starting to rattle the trees.

"Razim told you about the payment?"

"Yes. Are you going to do it yourself?"

"What? Oh, you mean the accident. No, of course not. I have someone better, a tourist." He looked up at the rain, only a thin drizzle coming through the banyan leaves. "You are sure your husband will remain asleep?"

I wasn't sure if he was testing me to see if I would speak truthfully to him, if Razim had told him about Halimah's powder or not. Not that Razim knew about Halimah, but he knew I had a powder from a bomoh. So I said simply, "Yes, I am sure." Then, feeling bolder once more at the memory of Halimah, I asked him if Razim had specified that he could only watch, that he was not to come near me or touch me.

He smiled, and that, too, I will always remember, for even someone so depraved can have a beautiful smile.

"That's what they like to do," he said. "They like to watch only. Come."

· · ·

THERE WERE FIVE others, besides Razim's uncle. We may as well call him Razim's uncle as any other name. You can hear from his speech he was not your usual kampong fellow, although he was Malay, or so he looked to me. The other five were foreigners, all with blond hair. I thought they were brothers. Perhaps they were, perhaps not. I couldn't tell them apart, except for one who had the grace to blush when I began undressing.

The other woman, I don't remember her face at all, but she was Eurasian, too. As it turned out, she was the reason the five brothers, the foreigners, were interested in our show, because of her operation, you see, because this other woman used to be a man and what the foreigners had paid for was to see what happened if a woman like that made love to another woman, to the kind of woman they themselves might make love to, a woman like me.

Yes, we touched wherever they wanted us to touch, as long as they kept their own hands away. It was only a show, my darling. Worse things than that can happen in this life, and worse things have already happened. All the wars that men wage among themselves, girls always get trapped in them, and yes, boys, too. Always the children, and often, women.

It was only a show, no longer than an hour. It wasn't hard to get through. All the while my gaze was fixed on the slope of the ceiling, or on the chinks between the planks of wood that made up the walls of the room. Only for one disturbing moment did I wonder if Razim was in the house, if perhaps this was his house, too, and then I managed to disentangle myself from the thought, and for the rest of the hour, my soul was sitting on the rooftop in the rain, drinking in my coming freedom in the wet dawn.

WAS THERE NO other way? The truth, as I've said, is seldom the first thing we see. Dust is all around us, not only in your dreams.

Once, two young men held down a child, prodded and poked into her as if she were a doll, choked her on her own vomit, and one of the men was already a father, and the other, his best friend, my Alvin. This happened, and there were no witnesses, only a brother who would never be forgiven for wandering away from his sister to watch some older boys playing soccer in the field next-door to the community center (the brother, five years old, had been told to stay with his sister, whose body would be found two weeks later), and only your mother, who when she became pregnant with you, began to dream of a girl lost in a field of sugar cane, who kept calling to her.

That was why your mother came home. She thought the girl was you, your soul waiting for you here. She didn't know about your sister until the two of you were born, your sister first, then you. The placenta tore when we pulled your sister out, leaving only a wrinkled scrap curled around her foot. But you came out slippery like a tadpole, and almost fully sheathed.

Why did I lie to Fatimah? Because this story now belongs to you, my darling.

Your grandmother, Valerie Nair, believed your sister had no heart, that the doctors had missed nothing, that there never was a heartbeat. You hear what I'm saying? Your sister was a stillbirth.

YOUR GRANDMOTHER, VALERIE, bathed her before the ambulance arrived. In an enamel basin, in frangipani water, on the floor of your mother's bedroom, away from the windows. She knelt over your sister's body and rubbed off the blood, peeling the placenta from your sister's foot and slipping it into her own pocket. We all saw it. Your mother, I, and Sister Rosalind, who also was there that night and had not yet decided to become a nun. Yes, they were close, Sister Rosalind and your mother. They were childhood friends, like you and Fatimah. Rose, Sister Rosalind was called in those days.

We had to change the water six times before it remained clean when we immersed your sister.

I took you from your mother when Rose—Sister Rosalind—who was watching by the windows, saw the ambulance arrive.

We were in the bathroom downstairs when the men entered your grandmother's house. You were already asleep, a limp and heavy wonder in my arms, your hot breath blowing over the hair on my skin. You flinched when the men went up the stairs, and I heard you whimper, but when they came back down, carrying your mother and your sister, you were quiet.

Your mother's bedroom was already cleaned up when the men saw it. They didn't know about you, and all they would have heard if they had been listening on the stairs would have been the water I had left running in the bathroom sink, a rhythm to keep you soothed, a murmuring like your mother's blood, to make you think her muscle was nestled against your head, her bones cradling you.

Neither Rose nor I asked your grandmother that night what she was going to do with the piece of placenta in her pocket, and later it seemed to me, as it must have to Rose, that some questions should be left alone, that perhaps it was better for you not to know everything.

Now you've kachaued all of that, my darling, you and your grandmother, as perhaps is the inevitable outcome. No doubt, she still has it, that piece that was stuck to your sister's foot locked away in one of her lacquered boxes, tucked between the pages of your mother's last book, the one your mother was trying to finish writing before you were born, the one she was afraid her American publisher would not accept and yet she had written it anyway, for you.

Rose and I searched high and low for it that night, while your grandmother sat outside with you on the patio. Perhaps some of what you dream is hers, the trace of eau de cologne from her skin, the taste of limes and jasmine in the dark. It was the only time I would break my promise to your mother to keep you away from your grandmother until you were grown up. Because your grandmother was already falling ill—that was why your mother gave you to me, and why I let your grandmother hold you that night. Her mind had already begun to send words out of her mouth that made no sense. What she believed about your sister having no heart, about there being a hollow space in her rib cage where the heart was supposed to be. She was sure she had felt the hollow space when she bathed your sister.

If she approaches you again, ask her for that book, your mother's book. See what she says. Rose and I never found it. I am sure your grandmother has it. But don't follow her into the house, my darling, if only to honor your mother's last request.

No matter if some of the neighbors see you. They won't recognize you. You do not have your mother's face.

LISTEN TO THE wind outside. Nothing so beautiful as the freedom of the wind, the music it makes roaming through the branches of the banyans. Hear how it slides between the leaves, sprinkling what we have been into the night, the ashes of our skin, droplets of what you and I have spoken and will speak, here in our time together, here a humming consonant, there an open vowel, our memory gathered and looped like necklaces and bracelets over the earth's own blades of grass.

We are the earth's own, my darling. Hear how your mother is not lost, never lost. Hear which beads in the wind are hers.

Your grandmother may have used Halimah's powder on your grandfather, and I was not the only one who had always suspected it. You understand our silence now?

Now go and let Malika know we will be ready to eat soon. Then come back and bring another candle. No, leave the windows open. It will not rain, not tonight.

GLOSSARY

SINGLISH, THE ENGLISH vernacular of Singaporeans, is a hybrid language formed from the blending of King's English, Hokkien, and Malay, languages spoken by this island's largest communities following British colonization. Hokkien is properly termed a dialect, originating in the Fukien province in China. Malay is indigenous to the region, and while the path of its formation remains uncertain, Arabic and Sanskrit influences are evident.

aiya	interj. *Hokkien*. Used to express disappointment or mock exasperation.
alam	n. 1. *Arabic*. the world; the universe. 2. nature. — adj. knowing best: *Allahu~*, God who knows best.
alamak	interj. Used to express surprise.
apa	adj. 1. what. 2. *buluh~*, a dwarf bamboo.
api	n. fire; light.
bapa	n. father.
betul	adj. correct; true; straight.
bodoh	adj. stupid; dull; simple.
bomoh	n. A healer and practitioner of black magic, traditionally male.
buat	v. doing; making.
bukan	adv. not; there is not; it is not.
bunga	n. 1. a flower. 2. an ornamental pattern or design.
bunga kubur	n. *Arabic*. flower of the tomb.
char kway teow	n. *Hokkien*. fried rice noodles.
Che'	n. Miss or Mrs.
chiku	n. 1. *Manilkara zapota*, synonymous with *Achras zapota*, commonly known as the sapodilla, a tree culuvated troughout the tropical regions of the world. 2. the fruit of this plant (the sapodilla fruit, also known as *níspero* in Latin America and *naseberry* in the West Indies).
dalang	n. the story-reciter (who also works the figures) at a Malay shadow play; the author (in stories written for use in the shadow play).
dang-ki	n. *Hokkien*. A Chinese spirit medium.
dia	pron. he; him; she; her; it; they (if clear from context); *orang*, they.
gila	adj. mad; insane.
habis	v. done; finished — adv. entirely; done for.
haji	n. holy man.
itu	pron. that; those. — adj. that; those.
jangan	v. don't.
kachau	v. confuse; disturb.
kampong	n. village; rural community.
kangkung	n. a white or pink flowered convolvulus.
kechil	adj. 1. small. 2. younger. 3. inferior.

kena	*v.* contact (to come into contact with, or to be brought into contact with).
kris or keris	*n.* a Malay dagger, which may be short or long, straight or wavy, shaped for close fighting and fast movements and maneuver.
kubur	*n. Arabic.* 1. tomb. 2. *bunga* ~, the cemetery flower; the frangipani.
kulit	*n.* 1. skin. 2. rind; peel; crust; shell; husk; bark. 3. leather.
lah	*def. art. Informal.* Used to emphasize the word to which it is appended.
lalang	*n.* Imperata cylindrica, a long grass common in Malaysia, Singapore, and Indonesia. — *v. lalu* ~, passing to and fro.
langsuir	*n.* a vampire.
lari	*v.* running; fleeing.
makan	*v.* 1. eat; consume. 2. wear away. 3. take effect or be affected by.
masok	*v.* enter.
mahu	*v.* want; wish; desire.
nya	*adj.* The possessive form of the third person. — *pron.* Used to indicate the one or ones belonging to him, her or it.
nyonya	*n.* 1. Straits Chinese woman. 2. the queen, at cards.
pandan	*n. Pandanus amaryllifolius*, commonly known as the screw pine or screw palm. The natural distribution of the genus extends from Africa and Madagascar, through Southeast Asia and Australia to the Pacific Islands. Food cooked in pandan leaves has a fragrant flavor.
pantang	*v.* considering something to be a harbinger or vessel of bad luck.
parang	*n.* a long Malay knife, shaped for cutting grass or chopping trees, used also as a weapon.
pekak	*adj.* 1. hard of hearing. 2. deaf. 3. less strong than.
Peranakan	*n.* Straits-born Chinese, as referred to by Malays.
pontianak	*n.* a vampire that preys on women in labor and on children.

puchat	*adj.* pale (as a result of shock or illness).
pulot hitam	*n.* black rice pudding.
punya	*adj.* Used with a noun or pronoun to indicate possession.
puteh	*adj.* white.
sambal	*n.* very spicy chili condiment.
sampai	*v.* 1. arrive; reach. 2. attain. — *prep.* up to the time of.
sudah	*adv. Persian.* already.
t'ak or tidak	*adv.* 1. no. 2. not.
takut	*adj.* fearful.
tau suan	*n. Hokkien.* yellow lentil pudding.
tengok	*v.* see; look.
terkejut	*intr.* v. startled.
ulu	*adj.* rural.
wayang	*n.* 1. a traditional theatrical performance, whether by living actors or shadow puppets; play; drama. 2. *ikan* ~, a fish.

ACKNOWLEDGMENTS

I WANT TO express my deepest gratitude to Shalini Puri and Amrita Puri, whose loving and insightful reading kept this book from disappearing. To Carlos Cañuelas Pereira, Katheryn Rios, Geeta Kothari, Mark Kemp, Michelle Wright and Virginia Nugent, who brought me solace, silence and food. To Edward Washington, who tended so many fires in the early stages. To Lydia Fakundiny, for her example of precision. To Toi Derricote, for her constant faith. To my colleagues and students in the English department at the University of Pittsburgh, especially Mariolina Salvatori, James Seitz, Nancy Glazener, Gerri England, David Bartholomae, Catherine Gammon, Richard Ing and Jennifer Kwon Dobbs, whose help and encouragement were indispensable.

Thanks to the Small Grants Program of the University of Pittsburgh Central Research Development Fund and the Hewlett International Grants Program at UCIS for their support. To C.M. Turnbull for his work in *A History of Singapore 1819–1988*, which provided the particulars of modern scholarship on the topic. To my editor Laura Hruska for her thoughtful suggestions, and my agent Alice Martell for her tenacity.

Thanks to my mother for my first library card. My father, who once insisted that human character without compassion was worth nothing. Butch and my cousins, for ghost stories. My brother, who graced our childhood with his humor. Caroline, Ah Lian and my Koko, for taking care of us.

Special gratitude and love to Christine Kanagarajah, Angela Yeo McKenzie and Mabel Ng, for inspiration and memory.